WOLF HALL

COMPANION

First published in the United Kingdom in 2020 by Batsford
43 Great Ormond Street
London WC1N 3HZ
An imprint of Pavilion Books Company Ltd

ISBN: 9781911358619

A CIP catalogue record for this book is available from
the British Library.

25 24 23 22 21 20
10 9 8 7 6 5 4 3 2 1

Printed in Turkey

This book can be ordered direct from the publisher at the website
www.pavilionbooks.com, or try your local bookshop.

Distributed in the United States and Canada by Sterling Publishing Co., Inc.
1166 Avenue of the Americas, 17th Floor, New York, NY 10036

FSC
www.fsc.org
MIX
Paper from
responsible sources
FSC® C111584

WOLF HALL

COMPANION

Lauren Mackay

BATSFORD

CONTENTS

INTRODUCTION

'So now get up.'
(*Wolf Hall*)

The violent blows of his father leave the young Thomas Cromwell sprawled on his side, his bruised body finding little comfort from the dirty cobblestones. The smell of blood and beer infuses the air of the Putney blacksmith's yard. In the distance he hears shouting, but all Thomas can focus on is his father's large boot, placed inches away from his head, the stitching tying the boot together unravelling from the violent movements.

Everything shifts out of focus, yet somehow he stands up and hobbles to the house of his older sister, Kat Williams. Married into the Williams family, whose influence stretches no further than Wimbledon, but seemingly powerful to a boy who has never ventured beyond Putney, Kat has escaped their abusive father but can offer little protection when Walter inevitably comes to rage at the door demanding that Thomas return home. Thomas realizes that he must leave Putney but begins to dream a little bigger. He wonders if somewhere in Europe there is a war raging and imagines becoming a soldier.

He flees to the port of Dover where he encounters three Lowland cloth merchants. In return for helping them carry their bundles on board the boat crossing the English Channel, they take him along as a member of their party. Throughout the journey he reveals the details of his life to them: stories of his childhood, his father's abuse and illegal activities. The men are horrified at how badly the English treat their children. When the ship docks in Calais they part ways, the men tell Thomas that if he ever needs a bed and hearth, he will be welcome. But the young Cromwell will not stop till he finds a war. As he is greeted by the sight of the vast open sea for the first time, he kisses the holy medal his sister has given him for protection and drops it into the sea.

With this unsentimental introduction to the 16th century, and to the boy who would become one of the most infamous individuals of the period, so begins Mantel's opus *Wolf Hall* with an undeniable freshness (stale beer and blood in the air notwithstanding) and honesty, portending a darker, grittier world than we are accustomed to.

The lure of historical fiction, as author Margaret Atwood suggests, is the lure of time travel. Every generation or so, across various forms of media, the Tudor kings and queens are reimagined and refashioned. Readers don't require a new ending, for we know Henry VIII's songbook all too well. What we want is to immerse ourselves in the glamour, opulence and infinite intrigues and trysts of the Tudor court, all rich and beguiling thrills for our imaginative senses. In most novels of the period, we are invited to marvel at the majesty and sophistication of Henry's palaces; partake in the extravagant, multi-course feasts of beast, fish and fowl; to feel the weight of jewel-encrusted velvet gowns brushing across stone floors; and catch the advisors jostling for power as they scheme and squabble behind the doors of the Privy Chamber. And just beyond all this we can witness the towering figure of Henry as he pursues his women into the royal bedchamber, beckoning the reader, where, on occasion, bodices are ripped.

Hilary Mantel's compelling trilogy – *Wolf Hall* (2009), *Bring Up the Bodies* (2012) and *The Mirror and the Light* (2020) – and their stage and screen adaptations, invite us into a world of religion, politics, international affairs and Tudor governmental reform. Mantel treads the same ground as historian and novelist alike, but her construction of the past allows for an entirely new perspective. As Mantel has said, while the Tudor period remains vigorously contested for historians, to a general audience it is a rich vein of endless escapades and melodrama, with surprising tableaux of light entertainment. There are bookshelves full of novels about Henry VIII and his six queens, but in Mantel's words, 'change the viewpoint, and the story is new'. It is not Henry who leads us through the corridors of court and power, nor one of his legendary queens. Instead we follow Mantel's 'He, Cromwell', whom the foremost Tudor historian, Geoffrey Elton, famously declared was 'not biographable'.

FINDING CROMWELL

With the fall of Cardinal Wolsey, Thomas Cromwell emerged to become one of the most powerful men of the Tudor age, whose career has divided historians ever since. While he has always been a pivotal figure in Tudor politics, some historians have viewed him as a morally dubious character who drew around him sinister spheres of court officials and hangers-on. The Cromwell of *Wolf Hall* is an astute observer of the machinations of the court, clever and calculating, at least until he flies too close to the royal personages and himself gets burned.

Yet of the enigmatic historical figure that was Thomas Cromwell, we know very little, which seems to be exactly how he wanted it. For Cromwell, information and knowledge were forms of currency, to be traded for leverage and influence with those around him; a guarded man when it came to his own background, he successfully cultivated an air of mystery, perplexing friend and enemy alike. He has remained elusive to many historians as there is a distinct lack of textual evidence to define him. Furthermore, elements of Cromwell's legacy are lost to history owing to the deliberate destruction of years of his accumulated papers and letters following his execution, and the passage of time. There is a definite one-sidedness to surviving documents from Cromwell: as historian Professor Diarmaid MacCulloch notes, only the 'in-tray' survives. This largely comprises letters addressed to him of a personal nature, or in his various official roles up to and including his highest appointment, as Chief Minister. We have so few letters in his own hand, MacCulloch notes, that Cromwell's 'own voice is largely absent'. And it is precisely in the absence of evidence that an impressive mythology has evolved over the centuries. As Mantel's Cromwell prophesizes: 'Strive as I might, one day I will be gone. When the time comes I may vanish before the ink is dry. I will leave behind me a great mountain of paper, and those who come after me will turn the page over and write on me.'

And we have. As Mantel has it, the living chase the dead.

FACT AND FICTION

Even during his lifetime, Cromwell's friends and enemies struggled to explain how a man with such an obscure, if not outright questionable, background could rise so high at the English court. Some contemporary sources attributed Cromwell's elevation to a single conclusive meeting he had with Henry VIII in 1530. This was when Cromwell presented a blueprint which would allow the King to take control of the Catholic Church in England, improve its administration and, most importantly, end Rome's dominance and interference in matters of state. Henry wanted an annulment of his marriage to Katherine of Aragon to be determined in England and not by the Pope in Rome, who was far less favourable to the annulment. Our main sources for this breakthrough moment in the long and exasperating negotiations are Imperial ambassador to the Tudor Court, Eustace Chapuys, Cardinal Reginald Pole, and John Foxe. All three believed that Cromwell, in one masterful stroke, had ingeniously solved Henry's marital problems, thus ensuring his promotion within the government, and forever endearing himself to the king.

Cromwell would become involved in some of the darkest events of Henry VIII's reign, all of which have left an indelible stain on his character for many historians, while Henry seems to have escaped much of that censure. Nineteenth-century historians unsurprisingly found Cromwell guilty of leading Henry astray, describing him variously as: 'the most despotic minister who had ever governed England;' a 'notorious chief minister;' and a 'supreme master of the bloody game of faction politics'. As one modern Tudor historian noted, 'for mafia-style offers you can't refuse, look no further than Thomas Cromwell.'

Historian Geoffrey Elton argued that Cromwell was the architect of radical changes in legal, political, social, economic and religious life. More recently, Professor Diarmaid MacCulloch, in his comprehensive biography *Thomas Cromwell: A Revolutionary Life* (2018) presents quite a formidable reappraisal of the man and minister, leading us through a tangle of surviving documents to show how this son of a Putney blacksmith modernized Tudor bureaucracy and politics. In fiction, Robert Bolt's memorable play *A Man for All Seasons* (1960) and the movie based on it (1967), present Cromwell as an accomplished villain and a royal hit-man. In the movie *Anne of a Thousand Days* (1969), Cromwell is depicted as brutish thug, a shrewd fixer and henchman for the king. The popular British TV Series *The Tudors* (2007) depicts Cromwell as a ruthless minister, a smirking, Machiavellian-style schemer, though with something of a conscience.

Cromwell is neither hero nor villain in Mantel's work, and she deftly explores his psyche, from the thrashing at the hands of his father through to his extraordinary rise as the King's indispensable 'fixer'.

A NEW CROMWELL

While historical facts are non-negotiable, Mantel weaves a narrative of fact and fiction from one of the most famous periods in history. She sculpts entire conversations from the dispatches of the period, extracts references to individuals and quirky expressions from fragments within communiqués and fills the gaps in the historical record with plausible motives and interior monologues, She is always reaching for that distinctive tone she came to recognize as 'He, Cromwell', asking us to look beyond his image as the King's enforcer, at the same time reminding us that this is fiction. The power of a persuasive narrative is that it allows us to identify with great figures of the era. And that is the double-edged sword of historical fiction – long after we forget the exact details and dates, we still hold our emotional tie to the characters we loved, and loathed.

Mantel guides us through the labyrinthine corridors of power in this first dedicated fictional portrait of Henry VIII's chief minister. At first he watches from the sidelines but he is by no means an impartial observer – he is making mental notes, remembering everything. He is calculating – 'What's in this for me?' – and cynical; for he has learned to be suspicious of peoples' motives. Along the way he is just a man with a family, with all the vicissitudes that entails, as he endures personal tragedy, great grief and self-doubt.

Mantel reimagines Cromwell's consciousness, and through his eyes we see the major players of the Tudor pantheon: Henry VIII, Anne Boleyn and Cardinal Wolsey among others, effectively upending the traditional tropes. Anne Boleyn is darker and more brittle than she has usually been drawn, Cardinal Wolsey is more than a haughty mountain of scarlet, and Thomas More is not a man for all seasons but one of cruel conviction. Controversial portraits indeed, but Mantel is merely asking us to 'consider this'. From his cell in the Tower, the real Cromwell wrote to Henry, admitting that 'I have meddled in so many matters under your highness, that I am not able to answer them all.' Certainly the extent of Cromwell's involvement in some of the most extraordinary and violent moments of Henry VIII's reign may never be truly known. Mantel blends fact and fiction – people, personalities, and motivations have been imagined and embellished for dramatic effect, interwoven with documentary evidence. History has provided us with the how and what, but Mantel has made her own suggestions as to *why*.

This companion presents the main events, places and themes rendered in Mantel's monumental trilogy; however, with such a vast *dramatis personae*, not every character makes an appearance. And while Mantel's Cromwell may have written 'the book called Henry', this work is not concerned with the monarch, but rather the court and the people whose lives revolved around him, aiming to enrich the reader's understanding of Mantel's works and the history beneath it, while threading through the historical narrative of this endlessly fascinating period.

I
RISING
FORTUNES

CROMWELL'S EARLY LIFE

In a generation everything can change.
(*Wolf Hall*)

In August of 1485, likely the very year Thomas Cromwell was born, two men fought at the heads of their armies on Bosworth Field in Leicestershire: King Richard III of the House of York and his challenger, Henry Tudor. Within hours, Richard III lay dead on the battlefield, his 10,000-strong army scattered. The battle followed Richard's victory over the House of Lancaster in the Wars of the Roses, the dynastic struggle that had plunged the country into civil war for decades. Appreciating the gravitas of the moment, Lord Stanley, Henry's step-father, rushed to his side and placed the golden circlet that had been attached to Richard's helmet on his head, thereby proclaiming him Henry VII, King of England and Wales.

Rewards and titles would flow to those whose exceptional valour had won this victory, but Henry required a new age for England. Although he and later historians would defend the legitimacy of his claim to the throne, he recognized that only a successful kingship would truly justify his seizing the crown. For now he needed to secure the best counsel around him, not just from the ranks of the nobility that had served previous kings, but men of talent and education, chosen on merit rather than birth, to lead his government and bring peace and prosperity to his kingdom. Henry VII's new way of doing business opened up career opportunities to many in the Tudor equivalent of a civil service. These new men serving the Tudors rose from amongst the middle ranks of town and country to become some of the most famous Tudor personalities.

Under Henry's son, Henry VIII, the court became a stock exchange for courtiers craving advancement where they could list their personal value and demonstrate their skills; a change in their status could bring power, estates and titles. Yet even in a world of opportunity, few could have imagined that Thomas Cromwell of Putney, son of a blacksmith and brewer, would become indispensable to the king.

As discussed in the introduction, exactly how this happened is something of a mystery, for Thomas Cromwell's trajectory from the grimy streets of Putney to the Privy Council is not well documented; he was guarded about his early life, leaving us with few textual traces from which we can construct his backstory, but from which, in the right hands, an interesting fictional narrative might be woven.

Cromwell is an Anglo-Saxon name, originating in Ireland and Nottinghamshire, and it is likely our Thomas was distantly related to the Lords Cromwell who owned the beautiful moated, red-bricked Tattershall Castle in Lincolnshire. The Cromwell name even graced royal records, as in Ralph de Cromwell, third Baron Cromwell, who fought alongside Henry V when he defeated the French at the famous battle of Agincourt. In 1420 he was one of the commissioners who assisted Henry V in the negotiations for the Treaty of Troyes, which ensured that upon the death of Charles VI of France, the French crown would pass to the English king. During the reign of Henry VI, he was appointed Lord Treasurer of England. So, the family had consorted with those of power and prestige at the English court, and our Cromwell would not be the first of his name to achieve success.

Cromwell's particular line, however, was of the yeoman class, forever struggling to break through class barriers. Their moment came when Cromwell's grandfather, John Cromwell, a successful business owner from Ireland, moved the family including his two sons John and Walter to Putney in London.

With Cromwell, there was a degree of gentility mixed with the mercantile; he enjoyed describing himself as a former ruffian, cultivating an image of a low-born man made good, something his enemies would later sneer at and use against him. Although Cromwell may have wanted to retain an air of mystery about his life, we have four key sources, individuals who, as we shall see, took a keen interest in his progress and were able to flesh out his early years: ambassador Eustace Chapuys, who served for almost two decades at the Tudor Court; Matteo Bandello, a contemporary Italian writer, soldier, monk, and sometime bishop; Cardinal Reginald Pole; and protestant martyr John Foxe.

Eustace Chapuys was sent to act as Katherine of Aragon's divorce lawyer by Charles V, her nephew, to mediate between Queen Katherine and King Henry. His official position at Henry's court was Imperial ambassador so it is surprising that, as we shall see, he and Cromwell developed a close personal relationship.

Chapuys was a prolific letter writer, sometimes completing up to ten a day. Many were to Charles V and to Charles' aunt, Margaret of Austria, and others including his friend and confidant, Nicolas Perrenot de Granvelle, a politician and ambassador from Burgundy.

Chapuys, like all ambassadors, had to be well-informed about the convictions and motives of courtiers, especially those who held sway over the monarch. Assembling fragments of Cromwell's life and lineage was a particular challenge for Chapuys given the secrecy surrounding his background. But Chapuys did discover that he was imprisoned briefly for crimes unknown, before travelling to Flanders, Rome and other Italian cities. There may be some truth to the imprisonment story as much later, in 1516, Cromwell was involved in a legal dispute against the sheriffs of London who intended to imprison him for an outstanding debt. In one report to Charles V, Chapuys wrote that Cromwell's uncle had been a cook for William Warham, Archbishop of Canterbury, and his father Walter was an unsuccessful and impoverished blacksmith who had lived, toiled and died in Putney. This was rather innocent information which Cromwell himself might have revealed in a rather unguarded moment, or on one of those occasions when he would wallow in regret about his misspent youth, when he was 'rather ill-conditioned and wild.'

WALTER CROMWELL

Thomas may not have obsessed over his lineage, but in *Wolf Hall* it is an obsession for his father Walter. His savage beating of son Thomas that opens the novel turns us against Walter and forever wins us over to Thomas's side. Walter's life is said to have been full of disappointment and bitterness, eating away at him as his dreams of reclaiming the wealth and status of his ancestors were shattered: 'Walter thinks he's entitled. He'd heard it all in his childhood: the Cromwells were a rich family once, we had estates.'

When we look at the history, there is some confusion, unhelpfully perpetuated by historians. Historical references reveal that Walter had various interests, from farming and commercial beer brewing to woollen clothmaking. One historian added blacksmithing to his curriculum vitae, even that he had served as a farrier, a smith who shoes horses, and that he served in Henry Tudor's contingent at the Battle of Bosworth. Still other historians ascribed a certain degree of lawlessness. Among our 20th-century historians it was Roger Merriman who disparaged Walter's character, describing him as a 'most quarrelsome and riotous character' and 'not seldom drunk'. It only takes one reference to cause a veritable flood, and soon later historians, building upon these foundations, speculated that Walter was not only a violent man but a criminal; after all, he had a record of being fined for assaulting a man, convicted of brawling, fraud and repeatedly fined for breaking the assize of ale, which meant he sold watered-down merchandise. But the meticulous examination of court records by Professor MacCulloch has rescued Walter from this last accusation, noting that the frequency of the fines points to a 'routine, manorial system of licensing ale selling, couched in terms easy to mistake as a fine in the modern sense.'

But MacCulloch had drilled down further to find every historian's dream: real evidence in the form of a letter written to Thomas Cromwell in 1536 from Anthony St Leger, a protégé of Cromwell's who would later become Lord deputy of Ireland. It thanks Thomas for all that he has done, and praises Walter for his goodness and assistance. Far from being the lawless drunk we have heard about, Walter was a successful local tradesmen and member of the community, as reflected in his frequent calls to serve as a juryman and his appointment as constable of Putney, suggesting he was well thought of in the community.

This has resulted in a debate regarding Cromwell's parentage, suggesting that it may be more complicated – was Walter Thomas' biological father? Writing of Cromwell's years in Italy, his Italian contemporary Matteo Bandello recounted a scene in which Cromwell described himself as 'the son of a poor cloth shearer', which is seemingly confirmed by Reginald Pole in his *Apologia ad Carolum Quintum* (1539). John Foxe, however, was more succinct, writing that Cromwell was 'born in Putney or thereabouts, being a smith's son, whose mother married afterwards to a shearman'. Certainly the varying portraits – well-to-do brewer or poor blacksmith and cloth shearer – do not quite correspond.

Far more elusive, historically and in *Wolf Hall*, is Cromwell's mother, Katherine. She is rarely referred to in official records although Cromwell once made the unlikely claim that his mother was 52 when she gave birth to him. Her maiden name was Meverell, and she came from a well-to-do family. She and Walter lived in a small house that adjoined their brewery near Putney Bridge Road in London. They had three living children, with Thomas being the youngest, born sometime between 1483 and 1485. Whatever the nature of Cromwell's relationship with his parents, he remained close to his two older sisters, Katherine and Elizabeth; Katherine's son, Richard, later adopted the Cromwell surname and became a protégé of his uncle's.

Thomas Cromwell's family details continue to be debated among historians, but with so little evidence available, not to mention Thomas Cromwell's own conflicting stories, we may never have the full picture.

THOMAS CROMWELL
ON THE CONTINENT

Thus, in his growing years, as he shot up in age and ripeness, a great delight came in his mind to stray into foreign countries, to see the world abroad, and to learn experience; whereby he learned such tongues and languages as might better serve for his use hereafter.
John Foxe

It is unlikely that Cromwell impetuously left Putney for the Continent to escape his father; more likely, he secured employment abroad before he left London. In *Wolf Hall*, Mantel draws back the curtain on his time in Europe but only intermittently, allowing us glimpses of the years that really shaped him:

In the year before he came back to England for good, he had crossed and recrossed the sea, undecided; he had so many friends in Antwerp ... if he was homesick, it was for Italy ....

Diarmaid MacCulloch remarks that much of Cromwell's early career rested on his 'ability to be the best Italian in all England'. And Italy does loom large in Cromwell's life, a connection that began in 1503 when, in his early twenties, he joined an expedition to Italy as part of the French army, fighting the Spanish at the Battle of Garigliano, just south of Rome, on 29th December 1503. Mantel invokes the Italian connection when noting that Cromwell does have 'something of that dark glitter of the Mafia boss about him'.

The Italian peninsula became the battleground for the French Valois kings and the Habsburg monarchs, who for decades were engaged in bloody hostilities known as the Italian Wars (1494–1559) as they fought for control over the powerful and wealthy Italian states of Florence, Venice, Genoa, the Papal States, the Duchy of Milan and the kingdoms of Sicily and Naples. Cromwell may have found himself a war, along with many of the other mercenaries who sustained both armies, but he picked the losing side. His first experience of warfare ended in a decisive defeat for the French, sealing a Habsburg domination of southern Italy. From the humiliation of defeat upon the battlefield, Cromwell slowly made his way to the famed city of Florence. Even then the city lured in 16th-century merchants and tourists alike with its iconic buildings: the Cathedral of Santa Maria del Fiore and its magnificent dome by Filippo Brunelleschi; the medieval Ponte Vecchio spanning the

Arno river; and the nearby Pitti Palace, which the Medici family had coveted for so long and would purchase in 1549, consolidating their rule over this great city of the Renaissance.

The Frescobaldis of Florence

It was from the streets of Florence, Bandello tells us, that Francesco Frescobaldi, a member of a wealthy Florentine mercantile family, rescued the young Cromwell from a life of poverty. How this might have happened is a mystery, but we do know that Cromwell was fortunate to associate with Francesco, for the Frescobaldis had been a powerful family in Florence since the 13th century. Their business interests were considerable, extending even to England and the new Tudor king, Henry VII, with whom they enjoyed an informal arrangement whereby goods imported from the East were allowed to travel via England, thence to Florence, thereby circumnavigating the highly taxed papal-controlled routes. The Frescobaldis were in the wine business and a leading exporter to England; today this 700-year-old history continues and they are still a large producer of Tuscan wines.

The Frescobaldi family were well-connected and respected among the Florentine gentry, renowned for their hospitality and entertaining, thus providing Cromwell with an unprecedented entrée into a world of wealth and privilege. Florence was a sophisticated city of art, culture and commerce, home to some of Europe's leading personalities of the period – including Michelangelo, who received many commissions from the Frescobaldis.

Mantel's Cromwell fondly recalls his time in the Frescobaldi sphere of influence and there are only a few casual references where she allows Cromwell to briefly reminisce:

It's not so many years since the Frescobaldi kitchen in Florence; or perhaps it is, but his memory is clear, exact. He was clarifying calf's-foot jelly, chatting away in his mixture of French, Tuscan and Putney, when somebody shouted, 'Tommaso, they want you upstairs.'

In describing the scene, Mantel may have taken inspiration more from John Foxe's recollections of a young Cromwell encountering the new Pope, Giovanni di Lorenzo de' Medici, who became Pope Leo X. Cromwell was hired by the Merchant's Guild of our Lady in Boston, Lincolnshire, which had been a prosperous wool-trading community since the 13th century. His mission was to travel to Rome to petition the Pope to renew their authority to collect papal indulgences on behalf of the Guild; many religious communities relied on the income generated by indulgences and without the papal licence their revenues would run dry. The mission was successful because Cromwell understood how business worked, perhaps something he had learned at the home of the Frescobaldis. Whereas most petitioners had to wait for months to be heard, Cromwell researched Pope Leo's personal tastes and discovered that the Pope delighted in new and 'dayntie dishes'. While on a hunting trip, Leo X was intercepted by Cromwell who had been working on an offering of his own, and produced several culinary delights, including jelly, for the Pope. This was a masterful stroke which so pleased the Pope that the Guild's petition to renew the indulgences was immediately granted. Frescobaldi's description then of Cromwell is on the mark:

'*Quick-witted and prompt of resolution...and could dissemble his purpose better than any man in the world.*'

The Frescobaldi experience would have been a revelation for Cromwell, arousing a taste for the finer things in life, such as fine art and tapestries, which he collected. This son of a Putney blacksmith must have indeed puzzled those at Henry's court, for where could this man have acquired such intelligence, worldliness and sophistication?

The provincial world of Putney was far behind as Cromwell, now fluent in Italian, Latin and French, was entrusted with the business transactions on behalf of the family, joining Francesco whenever he travelled for business. Cromwell's last mission for the Frescobaldis took him to Venice where he and his master parted ways, though not on bad terms. Perhaps Cromwell had decided to broaden his world, and the 16 gold ducats and fine horse that Francesco gave Cromwell as a parting gift shows their close bond. Mantel may even be alluding to Cromwell's affinity with Florence when her Henry teases him in *Bring Up the Bodies*: 'Cromwell has the skin of a lily,' the king pronounces. 'The only particular in which he resembles that or any other blossom.' The lily is the historic emblem of Florence, a fitting symbol of loyalty to the Florentine family who had set him on the path to success.

ANTWERP

We know that Cromwell also spent a short time in Venice, where he worked as an accountant, but from here the story shifts out of focus once more. Cromwell likely followed the trade routes from Venice through the cities of Europe, eventually reaching the Netherlands where he would again assimilate the skills and machinations of local business in a new area of commerce, namely as a cloth merchant. Cromwell had honed his financial skills in Italy, but Antwerp was the perfect training ground for a merchant.

Antwerp sits on the right bank of the Scheldt river, a gateway to the North Sea, ensuring it would surpass its rival, the city of Bruges, as a major centre of trade and commerce in Europe. Governed by bankers who were forbidden to engage in any trade themselves, Antwerp was well-organized and full of lucrative industries: breweries that would later make the city synonymous with beer; sugar refineries that imported the highly sought-after raw product from Portugal and Spain; salt imported from France and shipped abroad; diamonds bought from Indian merchants that were cut in the city by highly skilled Jews who had fled the persecutions of the Iberian peninsula. Its major activity was its tapestry workshops, which evolved into the major marketplace for Flemish tapestry. Indeed, Antwerp was the centre of the luxury market where dealers traded in exquisite tapestries, English cloth, and high-quality silks from Italy, from where Pope Leo X would commission the finest examples for his rooms in the Vatican. Antwerp was the mercantile capital of Western Europe, a financial centre that launched a stock exchange in 1531, drawing bankers from England, France, Portugal, Italy and the nations of the Holy Roman Empire; London would have to wait another 40 years for the creation of its stock exchange.

These channels of international trade and commerce also brought new religious and humanist influences, with the wind of reform in Antwerp attributable to the city's pre-existing tensions with the Catholic Church. Cromwell worked as a clerk or secretary, possibly for English merchants, and would have been aware of all the trends and movements in the city, and is likely to have been influenced by the religious discourse flowing through the city. Mantel's Cromwell gazes up at one of Wolsey's tapestries and is reminded of a young woman he had loved in Antwerp. Incidentally, the woman would turn out to be the fictional Anselma as Cromwell discovers in *The Mirror and the Light*, but the real Cromwell would have focused on the value of that tapestry, which workshop made it (Arras or Tournai perhaps) and the going rate for a similar work.

A MERCANTILE EDUCATION

Cromwell knew the value of a practical education and contemplated sending his son Gregory to stay with Stephen Vaughan, a merchant in Antwerp. Cromwell once wrote to Vaughan, declaring 'You think I am in Paradise, and

I think in Purgatory.' But he did have a great affection for Antwerp and a certain nostalgia for the place where he achieved so much.

Cromwell's return to England was thought to be some time in 1513 or 1514, but the Boston Guild's records of Cromwell in Rome place him in Italy in 1517 and 1518, so we can surmise that he travelled between England and Europe on various business trips during those years. With so many years spent in Europe, it is not surprising that Cromwell's fluency expanded to include numerous languages, including French, Italian, German and Spanish, as well as the languages reserved for scholars and academics: Latin and Greek.

Mantel's Cromwell overhears several conversations in a variety of languages including Flemish Latin and Greek. Not all of the conversations are useful, Cromwell says to himself, but they are to be remembered.

CROMWELL THE LAWYER

Our lesson with Cromwell is that he can be an unreliable narrator, and so historians have looked to official records to unearth his early career, particularly his time as a lawyer. We have no evidence of where Cromwell might have received legal training or if he had formal training at all, but his years in some of the most important centres of trade throughout Europe were enough to recommend him, and by the early 1520s he was well-known throughout London's legal and mercantile spheres, both of which offered considerable opportunities for the lawyer and merchant. Cromwell was admitted to the Honourable Society of Gray's Inn, one of the four inns of court in London, which was a prerequisite should Cromwell wish to be called to the bar.

Gray's Inn is an important element of Cromwell's professional life in Mantel's series and was an important stepping stone for Cromwell, allowing him to take on several high-profile clients and to cultivate a legal network. He soon entered into the service of Thomas Grey, 1st Marquess of Dorset, the eldest son of Elizabeth Woodville and her first husband, Sir John Grey of Groby. Interestingly, Cromwell was not merely a legal advisor, but rather served in Grey's household, in charge of conveying private correspondence between Grey and his wife as well as Grey's younger brother George, and the matriarch of the household, Cecily Grey. This time is not alluded to in the series, but it is clear from letters written by the Marquess to Cromwell years after his service that Cromwell had been held in high esteem, and he would remain connected to the Greys throughout his life.

THE CROMWELL FAMILY
AT AUSTIN FRIARS

Sometime in 1515 Cromwell married the daughter of a fellow merchant, Henry Wykys, who had served as Gentleman Usher to Henry VII. Cromwell had already established himself as a successful merchant and lawyer, and took over the reins of Henry Wykys's business in the cloth and wool trade; marrying Elizabeth Wykys was a beneficial match. The couple lived at Cromwell's bustling property of Austin Friars, a monastic house in London, which they rented. Several tenements were built on the western side of the precinct and the friary also owned a number of properties just outside the precinct. With its 14 rooms set across three storeys, Austin Friars features throughout the series and is full of Cromwell relatives, in-laws, nieces, nephews and wards. Over the years Cromwell's neighbours in the building complex include the Holy Roman Emperor's ambassador Eustace Chapuys, French ambassadors, and the famed scholar Desiderius Erasmus, who – allegedly – left without paying his bill due to the poor quality of the wine served. It is within its walls that we are introduced to Cromwell's wife Liz and their children. In *Wolf Hall* Liz has been fleshed out and, in a sense, gives voice to the female population of England, many of whom protested Henry's cruel treatment of Katherine: abandoning your wife of over 20 years (for a younger woman) was something the wives of England could empathize with. Every woman in England would be against it, she says:

All women who have a daughter but no son. All women who have lost a child. All women who have lost any hope of having a child. All women who are forty.

Cromwell and his wife had three children, Gregory, Anne and Grace. Cromwell also had an illegitimate daughter, Jane (or Janneke in Mantel's series), following the death of his wife, but we know very little about her circumstances, or of her mother. Jane may have resided in the Cromwell household as she had contact with the Cromwell family because she spent some time living with Gregory Cromwell at Leeds Castle in 1539. There has been speculation about Cromwell's relationship with his wife, but evidence suggests a happy and close marriage.

When we need evidence to substantiate a claim, there is nothing better than correspondence. One surviving letter reveals a dutiful husband, not only requesting news, but also providing meat for the family, a 'fat doe'

which he had killed himself while out hunting. Cromwell also bought his wife expensive jewellery, including a sapphire ring and a gold bracelet worth £80 – or approximately £40,000 in today's currency. Both Cromwell and his wife corresponded with various merchants and hosted many suppers at their imposing home, all providing intimate glimpses of the couple, which Mantel brings beautifully to life as she conjures joyful family gatherings, loving and warm conversations between Cromwell and his wife in their bedchamber, and business meetings with his son Gregory, nephew Richard and Rafe Sadler, a young boy who Cromwell had taken as a ward.

Austin Friars was home to Liz's father and stepmother, Henry and Mercy Wykys; Liz's sister Johane Williamson and her husband John, and their daughter, Johane, who is often called Jo; Cromwell's niece, Alice; and the son of his sister Kat, Richard, who would later adopt the Cromwell surname. Cromwell sought educations for all three children as well as his son and ward.

... it's not a dynasty, he thinks, but it's a start.

Following Liz's death in 1529, Cromwell never remarried, despite the advice of friends who urged him to do so. At the very height of his power, it seemed that matrimony was never on the cards, and while one might imagine that dealing with Henry's endless matrimonial woes was enough to deter him, it is more likely that his choice to remain widowed was personal – perhaps he could not bear the thought of another wife living within the walls of Austin Friars.

CROMWELL AND THE CARDINAL

It is not clear how Cromwell, merchant and lawyer, moved from the Grey household to that of Cardinal Wolsey, but historians have several theories. Wolsey had a strong connection to the Greys: Thomas had met Wolsey while at Oxford and Thomas Grey's father had given Wolsey his first benefice. But there were others in the Grey circle, such as John Allen, a family friend, who appointed Cromwell conveyancer to handle the sale of a property in York to Wolsey in 1524, and by January 1525 Cromwell was leading several complex projects for the Cardinal. Mantel's Cromwell notes: 'Wolsey cannot imagine a world without Wolsey', but nevertheless, Wolsey had already begun to plan his legacy: twin Cardinal Colleges and his tomb.

Such projects required vast sums of money but Wolsey had targeted six monasteries in decline, some around Ipswich and Oxford, which could be converted to colleges. Wolsey appointed Cromwell to survey the properties, and when the plan proved feasible, he was appointed to do the same for 30 more religious houses, which would go towards the college precinct, or if they could be sold, the proceeds could fund building works.

Wolsey had commissioned the Italian Renaissance sculptor Benedetto da Rovezzano to design and construct his final resting place. Wolsey must have considered his legacy, having attained the position of the most important person in England next to the king. Working with a team of Italian sculptors, this would be a monument to Wolsey's status and power: a black stone surrounded by copper pillars, decorated by bronze statues. Cromwell's mastery of Italian made him indispensable. Wolsey's trust in Cromwell now accelerated as he oversaw every financial and artistic element of these tasks. At the time of his death, the tomb was incomplete, the location undecided, and his legacy lay in tatters.

RICHARD FOX

But to understand Wolsey, we need to go back. Before Thomas Cromwell, before the brilliant Wolsey, there was another political mastermind: Richard Fox.

Richard Fox was an Oxford-educated lawyer from Lincolnshire who had loyally served Edward IV but could not support Richard III's claim to the throne, and fled to the young Henry Tudor's side in Brittany. The two men forged an immediate rapport, a collaboration that would endure for the next 25 years, with Fox becoming indispensable to Henry VII. Fox masterminded and engineered the highly ambitious alliance between England and the power couple of Europe, Spain's Ferdinand of Aragon and Isabella of Castile, through the marriage of their daughter, Katherine of Aragon, to Prince Arthur. Following Arthur's untimely death in 1509, Fox ensured that the royal coffers retained the dowry by arranging her marriage to his younger brother, Henry VIII. Fox also negotiated the famous Anglo-Scottish alliance between Princess Margaret and James IV in 1503, one that decades later would see a Scottish king on the throne of England.

Following the death of Henry VII and the accession of Henry VIII, Fox continued to be counsel the young, pleasure-loving king and his wife. But Fox was a pragmatist and could be a ruthless and unscrupulous opponent, as evidenced by his involvement in the infamous downfalls of Henry VII's old councillors and hatchet men, Edmund Dudley and Richard Empson, who were executed within the first days of the new king's reign. Powerful and influential, Fox was involved in most of the business conducted in the kingdom, with Henry trusting him to make decisions when he was absent from court, earning him the soubriquet *alter rex* ('other king'), to the chagrin of many of country's nobles. It was Henry VIII who, having measured Fox's character, declared that Richard Fox was not a man to be underestimated, for he was, as his name implied, 'a fox indeed'.

Within this world of power, intrigue and patronage, Fox was also a supreme mentor, shaping the lives of two men in particular – Cardinal Thomas Wolsey and Stephen Gardiner. Wolsey would, of course, go on to mentor Thomas Cromwell, imparting the skills Fox himself had once wielded; their own success is part of Fox's legacy.

WOLSEY

The cardinal, at fifty-five, is still as handsome as he was in his prime.
(*Wolf Hall*)

A tall, impressive man, Wolsey was the gateway to Henry, and Henry relied completely on Wolsey: no two such significant figures could have been closer. He stood above the royal councillors, many of whom resented his power and influence; even foreign rulers were highly deferential in their letters to him, as if they were writing to a fellow monarch. Cardinal Thomas Wolsey was one of the wealthiest and most powerful men of the Tudor age; his magnificent estate, Hampton Court, was even coveted by the King of England. Wolsey is an integral character in the Tudor narrative, and thus has played no small part in the many Tudor novels, movies and television dramas. In *Wolf Hall* it is Wolsey who conjures ghosts from behind his desk – Henry VII, Richard III, Prince Arthur – reminding us that Wolsey lived through the last tumultuous years of the Wars of the Roses and the reign of the first Tudor monarch.

But we have only two contemporary narratives of Wolsey, each from a different perspective. The first is by the 16th-century London chronicler Edward Hall, who described Wolsey as a self-serving, duplicitous advisor who manipulated and controlled the young king, advancing his own personal and political agendas, his arrogance and corruption contributing to his own demise. The other account was by Wolsey's loyal and long-term servant George Cavendish, a not entirely impartial observer who apologized for Wolsey extravagances but stressed that he was a most loyal servant of the king. These accounts of Wolsey's life are really a response to a very narrow period of history that took place during the twilight of Wolsey's life and career, and which led to his own downfall. In either case, these depictions affirm our view of Wolsey, accentuated in his famous portraits: the rapacious, rotund cardinal, scarlet robes stretched across his portly belly, with pink, fleshy hands adorned with gold and jewels.

Mantel rejects the tired readings of Wolsey, and avoids drawing on his enemies to strike him with their grievances: Anne Boleyn or Thomas More, for example. Rather she relies on Cromwell's more sympathetic and charitable account of Wolsey by breathing life into the meetings between the powerful Lord Chancellor and his servant. In a non-linear narrative she delves first into Cromwell's years in Wolsey's service, then offers us glimpses of Wolsey's powerful nature through Cromwell's recollections. These insightful exchanges flesh out every element of Wolsey's character: most memorable is that he speaks in 'honeyed tones, famous from here to Vienna'.

In *Wolf Hall*, several courtiers refer disparagingly to Wolsey as a butcher's son or butcher's dog, common slurs used frequently of the Cardinal, who was not of the aristocracy. Nor was he of the nobility, but the evidence suggests that his father was a reputable grazier, therefore landowner, from Ipswich in Suffolk, who reared sheep for wool for the lucrative textile industry, a far cry from a butcher. The young Wolsey was a prodigy as he was accepted into Magdalen College, Oxford, in his early teens, graduating at 15 with a Bachelor of Arts degree in 1486, earning him the nickname 'boy bachelor'. In March of 1498, Wolsey was ordained a priest, but he soon turned to administration, entering the service of Richard Fox, loyal supporter and advisor to Henry VII, part of the Henry's inner circle, along with his mother Margaret Beaufort. Serving as secretary to Fox, Wolsey was trained in the art of foreign policy, and cultivated important connections with the younger courtiers of Henry VII's reign. According to historian Polydore Vergil, Wolsey made friends through 'singing, laughing, dancing and clowning about with the young courtiers', a rather prudish observation.

Wolsey's career is impressive: in 1514 he became archbishop of York, and then a year later was elected Cardinal. He was Lord High Chancellor of England between 1515 and 1529, a position in which Wolsey wielded almost as much power as the king, which inevitably angered almost everyone.

With the accession of the young King Henry VIII in 1509, Wolsey quickly eclipsed his mentor Richard Fox, as he moved closer to the centre of power. He became a father figure to the young king, over 20 years his junior, and took over most of the administrative tasks, for young Henry preferred more trivial pursuits. Indeed, among many historians there is the sense that Henry shirked his responsibilities or allowed himself to be governed. But as Tudor historian Geoffrey Elton once reasoned: 'a man who marries six wives is not a man who perfectly controls his own fate'.

What Wolsey did do beautifully was to cultivate the king's dual nature – young man, young monarch. Mantel illuminates Wolsey's most important role in Tudor history: his influence on foreign diplomacy. Wolsey's vision was to position England as a facilitator of peace in Europe, with France on one side and the Holy Roman Empire on the other. In the first years of Henry's reign, different factions with vested interests jostled to influence the young king, urging Henry to go to war with Scotland. It was Wolsey who made a countermove by reasoning that warring with the French would position Henry as a powerful leader on the European stage. This decision was quickly followed by Wolsey's first diplomatic triumph, namely to convince Henry to join Pope Julius II's Holy League in 1510, which would unite the Papacy, Venice and Spain against France. Wolsey masterminded almost all the ensuing diplomatic negotiations, but his greatest achievement was to organize the most highly anticipated, and now famous, event of Henry's reign. The Anglo-French summit – the Field of Cloth of Gold – between King Henry VIII of England and King Francis I of France, which took place between 7 and 24 June 1520 in the English Pale of Calais, was designed to usher in a new era of Universal Peace between France and England.

Wolsey's career and political life are well-documented, but Wolsey the man is difficult to read through the sources despite the abundance of surviving letters. We do know that he was a deeply passionate advocate for education, a lover of humanist literature, art, music and architecture, but these traits are often used as examples of his opulent lifestyle. Wolsey spent a fortune building his colleges, but his other projects, Hampton Court and York Place, later called Whitehall, were architectural masterpieces.

Mantel discovered something in Wolsey beyond the stereotype and the criticisms. Perhaps Wolsey is in greater need of rehabilitation, as Mantel knows there is vastly more to his circumstances and his stellar ascent to the golden centre of the Tudor court. Mantel's Wolsey reclines in his chair and picks apart the threads to reveal the history of England and the Tudors for his clever new assistant, Cromwell, an insider's account of how it all began.

THE TUDOR
DYNASTY

It only lasted three generations, but the Tudors are undoubtedly the best-known of all English royal dynasties. They ruled from 1485–1603 as the Middle Ages gave way to Early Modern Britain at the beginning of the 1500s. It was a time when everything started to shift, particularly the relationship between the people and their monarch, and the people and their God. The Tudors could not boast a strong claim to the throne – the line can be traced back to humble Welsh origins sometime during the 13th century – but their rise to prominence began two centuries later with Owen Tudor, a Welsh landowner, who fought in the armies of Henry V.

'These are old stories', he says, 'but some people, let us remember, do believe them'.

Wolsey tells the story of Henry V's Queen, Catherine of Valois, mother of Henry VI, who embarked on a relationship with Owen Tudor, Keeper of the Wardrobe. Doubt has always been cast over whether Owen and Catherine ever married, and even if they had wed, it would likely not have been recognized, as the Act of 1428 forbade any royal marriage without the consent of Parliament. Owen Tudor's relationship with the widowed queen took place during the vicious civil wars between the two dynasties and rival branches of the royal house of Plantagenet – York and Lancaster. In an age when heirs and spares could cause tensions within a royal family, there was no animosity between Owen and Catherine's two sons, Edmund and Jasper, and their royal half-brother. Both Jasper and Edmund served as loyal advisors to Henry VI, devoted to his Lancastrian cause, and in turn they were highly trusted and respected members of the King's inner circle.

Owen and his son Jasper also led troops at one of the most decisive battles of the Wars of the Roses, the Battle of Mortimer's Cross in February 1461. It was a Yorkist victory and, unfortunately for Owen Tudor, he was captured by the troops of the Yorkist Edward IV, and beheaded without ceremony.

As Cromwell notes to Wolsey in *Wolf Hall*:

'By your account, my lord, our king's Plantagenet grandfather beheaded his Tudor great-grandfather.' 'A thing to know. But not to mention.'

It was the first and last time a Tudor would be executed. From that point, Tudors would be the ones wielding the axe.

Of the remaining Tudor heirs, Edmund married the 13-year-old Margaret Beaufort, a great-granddaughter of John of Gaunt, son of King Edward III, which provided a tenuous claim to the English throne. Margaret's marital track record – four husbands – would almost rival her grandson's, the future Henry VIII. She would only have one child, Henry Tudor, born on 28 January 1457, at Pembroke Castle in Wales, three months after the death of his father. With the deaths of Henry VI and his only son, Edward, the child Henry found himself the sole surviving male Lancastrian heir, a dangerous position in a country currently ruled by a Yorkist king. Henry was taken by his uncle Jasper to the duchy of Brittany in France, where it seemed he would live the rest of his years in exile, although his mother Margaret never lost faith that her son would one day sit on the throne. Edward IV died unexpectedly on 9 April 1483, and left two very young sons. His heir, 14-year-old Prince Edward, was too young to take the throne without a regent, and sparring factions within the divided royal family swiftly chose sides: one supporting the king's widow, Elizabeth Woodville; the other the dead king's brother, Richard, Duke of Gloucester. Richard made a pre-emptive strike by declaring himself Lord Protector of the young Prince Edward and his 12-year-old brother, Richard, and removed them to the 'safety' of the Tower of London, where they were lodged in preparation for Edward's coronation. However, no plans were forthcoming and the children disappeared from their apartments in the Tower, never to be seen again. Their uncle, Richard, Duke of Gloucester, crowned himself Richard III in July 1483. Richard could never escape the suspicion that he murdered his nephews, and he was surrounded by enemies who turned to the only alternative, Henry Tudor.

In early 1485, Henry had the financial and military backing for an assault on England and King Richard; his fleet sailed along the heavily defended south coast of England, around Land's End, arriving at the entrance to Milford Haven near Pembroke in Wales. Twelve days later, as Richard's troops marched towards Leicester, the two armies met on Ambien Hill, near the town of Market Bosworth, on 21 August 1485. By the next morning, Richard III lay dead on the battlefield.

With the country ravaged by years of conflict, Lancastrians and Yorkists now looked for peace rather than war, led from the top by two women: Henry's mother, Margaret, and Edward IV's widow, Elizabeth Woodville. They accomplished a union of the red and white roses through the marriage of Henry Tudor and Elizabeth of York, eldest daughter of Edward IV. Now crowned Henry VII, he and Elizabeth began the glorious Tudor Age, which would last till the end of Elizabeth I's Golden Age.

Henry VII inherited a devastated economy and was therefore preoccupied with replenishing the coffers by careful budgeting and raising taxes, which earned him a reputation as austere and miserly. Henry VII was fiscally moderate and rarely indulgent, but he understood the power of display. He recognized the need to promote the magnificence of the monarchy, and he cultivated relationships with some of the finest European poets, philosophers and humanists of the age, some of whom were chosen as tutors for the king's sons, Arthur and Henry, and helped shape the future king's attitudes towards the arts. Musicians played in the dancing chambers and halls of Henry VII's palaces while king and court feasted and played chess and cards. Henry VII, like his son, enjoyed the traditional courtly pursuits of hawking, hunting, bowls and archery, though his aim deteriorated along with his sight, once accidentally shooting a farmyard rooster – in the wrong place at the wrong time – with his crossbow.

To add a sense of mythology to his royal claim, he declared that he had traced his lineage back to the famous King Arthur, and the legend of Camelot permeated the court, with Henry and Elizabeth naming their first-born son after his illustrious forebear. Arthur would be followed by Henry, Duke of York, and two daughters, Margaret and Mary. The very future of the Tudor dynasty rested on Arthur's shoulders. Henry VII was tremendously invested in Arthur's education, ensuring he had the best tutors, and from the time he could walk he was kept separate from his siblings and received a royal education that would prepare him for kingship.

HEIRS AND SPARES

It was decided that young Prince Arthur, the heir to the English throne, would marry the young, auburn-haired princess Katherine of Aragon, daughter of the Spanish Empire's ruling monarchs, Isabella of Castile and Ferdinand of Aragon. Katherine represented the future: an England finally looking towards Europe. Katherine and Arthur were moved to Ludlow Castle, which stood near the English border with Wales, but the marriage was short-lived, as Arthur died six months into the marriage, possibly of tuberculosis. It is often stated that Arthur was sickly throughout his youth, but there is no contemporary evidence to support this theory, with several accounts noting his skill at archery, hunting and dancing.

Henry, now the heir, would go on to marry his brother's wife, apparently certain that Katherine had never consummated her first marriage, and confident that a papal dispensation would be granted to allow it. Katherine and Henry VIII were married and crowned in 1509, both in love and destined to preside over a golden world. Their partnership lasted almost 20 years.

Yet for all his confidence, Mantel's Arthur hovers, like a spectre at Henry's feast, haunting the king. As we shall see, Katherine's first wedding night will eventually be put under the microscope for the whole country to peer at, and the memory of Arthur conjured up before the court:

'A ghost walks: Arthur, studious and pale. King Henry, he thinks, you raised him; now you put him down.'

Neither Wolsey nor Cromwell could have foreseen Henry's complicated love life: he loved until he fell out of love, usually with alarming speed. He spent years trying to get his marriage to Katherine annulled as she could not produce a male heir; his second Queen, Anne Boleyn, might have been the love of his life, but she could not bear him a male heir either; his next great love was Jane Seymour, of whom we shall hear more later; she was followed by Anne of Cleves, Catherine Howard and, finally, Catherine Parr – the latter two marriages occurring after Cromwell's death.

Nor would anyone ever have imagined that of the three Tudor heirs – Mary, daughter of Katherine of Aragon; Elizabeth, daughter of Anne Boleyn; or Edward, son of Jane Seymour – only Elizabeth, who became monarch in 1558, would rule for more than a short time. This could only have happened with some tragedy and a few missteps in the family. When Henry died on 28 January 1547, the nine-year-old Edward VI was crowned King.

Under Edward England experienced significant religious reforms, moving towards a modern Church of England, though there were signs that Edward might take after his father in terms of temperament. Sadly Edward died at the age of 15, but not before he rather arrogantly reversed his father's order of succession and created his own in order to prevent the country's return to Catholicism. Excluding his half-sisters, Elizabeth and Mary, Edward named Lady Jane Grey, the granddaughter of Mary Tudor and Charles Brandon, as heir to the throne. The country rebelled against this decision, having always loved Mary, and Jane was deposed by Mary nine days after becoming queen. Mary was the first Queen regnant of England and Ireland, though her reign was marred by civil and religious unrest, however, she does not deserve the title 'Bloody Mary'. After only five years on the throne, Mary also died, and against all the odds it was Elizabeth, who had been declared illegitimate by her own father at the age of three, who held the sceptre. Elizabeth is only a baby in *Bring Up the Bodies*:

The child Elizabeth is wrapped tightly in layers. Ginger bristles poke from beneath her cap, and her eyes are vigilant; he has never seen an infant in the crib look so ready to take offence.

Elizabeth would rule England for 45 years, ushering in a glorious Golden Age and surpassing that of her father, but she had no Tudor heir to whom she was able to bequeath the throne – of Henry's three children, none would further the family line.

Mantel's Wolsey reviews the history laid out before him, Henry's first marriage, meant to consolidate the Tudor's glorious legacy:

'And now? Gone. Or as good as gone: half a lifetime waiting to be expunged, eased from the record.'
(Wolf Hall)

After just over a century in power, Henry VIII's direct line ended, but the Tudor line survived through the offspring of his sister, Margaret Tudor, who married King James IV of Scotland, of the Scottish house of Stuart. The throne of England passed to their son, James V of Scotland, continuing the Stuart dynasty, which was uninterrupted through to the 18th century, ironically enjoying greater longevity than the Tudors. Nevertheless, the Tudors remain one of the most extraordinary threads in the fabric of English history.

THE TUDOR COURT

We all know that there was a Court, and we all use the term with frequent ease, but we seem to have taken it so much for granted that we have done almost nothing to investigate it seriously.
(Geoffrey Elton)

There are countless fictional portrayals of the Tudor court, but what did it look like and how was it was structured? The Tudor court was essentially wherever the monarch, his household and retinue of high-ranking officials resided. It was the focal point of power, patronage and pleasure. But it was not a fixed location, as Henry VIII had numerous royal residences, and wherever he chose to reside became the court. Being constantly on the move allowed each palace to be cleaned, and eased pressure on the land and the various royal parks, allowing the game to be replenished. Henry VIII had over 60 estates; each palace and castle served as the seat of government while the king resided there. It might house thousands of individuals, from nobles and courtiers to servants. Wealthy and powerful families had their own apartments within the palaces, having furnished these rooms with their own tapestries and furniture. Crucially, these rooms also had their own closed stool, or privy, so individuals would not have to use communal facilities. Other courtiers had small rooms and would dine in public in the great hall.

Royal palaces were a maze of rooms, designed to restrict access to the king. Traditionally, the court was based on the centuries-old concept of a Great Hall – a single hall where the monarch heard petitions, consulted his advisors, feasted and danced. A slightly less public Presence Chamber was added, in effect a throne room, where business was conducted, foreign ambassadors would be admitted for an audience, and councillors would have state papers signed. The medieval system had these two chambers but Henry VII preferred the Italian model, which included private rooms for the monarch to conduct affairs of state in peace, uninterrupted by the court. Henry VII created the Guard Chamber, which was guarded by yeomen, as well as the innermost room within the Court, the Privy Chamber – private royal apartments where only the select few where allowed to attend the king. These chambers were run by the Gentlemen of the Privy Chamber, who attended to the king's every need, rising at dawn to help him dress, attending him throughout the day, and who would sleep just outside on pallets or folding beds. The Privy Chamber marked the private and public life of the monarch, and at the centre of this was the Groom of the Stool – he alone was permitted to enter the small room just off the bedchamber to attend the monarch's ablutions, even wiping the royal bottom. We come to know Henry's Grooms of the Stool, Henry Norris and Thomas Culpepper, very well through Cromwell's eyes. Both men would have slept at the foot of the King's bed, and in the morning would confer with the king to decide where he would hear Mass, when he wished to dine, and what activities he would like to pursue during the day. These decisions, made in the privacy of the inner sanctum, would ripple out towards the rest of the court, and set the palace in a flurry of activity.

Each palace consisted of two main divisions: the household proper, which was the *domus providencie*, presided over by the Lord Steward; and the *domus regie magnificencie* or 'above stairs', which was under the control of the Lord Chamberlain, and further sub-divided into the King's household and the Queen's household.

DOMUS REGIE MAGNIFICENCIE

This lay at the very heart of the Tudor court. Orbited by courtiers and members of the nobility and gentry, the Great Hall and chambers of court came under the jurisdiction of the *domus regie magnificencie*, where most fictional portrayals take place, and all the Tudor players can be located. Both chambers were bristling with individuals from either end of the spectrum, from gentlemen ushers, grooms, pages and chaplains to cupbearers. There was a strict and organized hierarchy as, for the most part, the whole court was always on show.

DOMUS PROVIDENCIE

The *domus providencie* was another world. Below stairs, this section was responsible for all practical elements of court life. The *domus providencie* was not one unit but rather several departments, all of which had their own hierarchy and head of operations, and these men would report to the Lord Steward. Departments included the almonry, bakehouse, cellar and kitchen, the acatry (which provided meat, fish and salt), the poultry (which provided fowl, lamb and eggs), the scullery (which took care of all the dishes and pots), the woodyard (which provided all wood for fires as well as wood for tables in the Great Hall), the spicery, the chaundry, and the confectionary (which was in charge of all the desserts and sweetmeats for the court).

Court Life

It was essential that differences in rank were observed, and that everyone abided by the sumptuary laws, which dictated one's life, from what one could wear and eat to what one could own. At court you were usually served two meals a day, dinner, served mid-morning after Mass, and supper, late in the afternoon. Your rank dictated how many dishes you could be served, and where you could be seated. In the Great Hall there were strict rules of dining etiquette. Each courtier provided his own utensils – a knife and spoon – with courtiers of higher rank also having a linen napkin, which they draped over their left shoulder. Courtiers could not blow their noses at the table, scratch themselves, break wind, spit or put bones back on a plate.

The Tudor diet was almost 80 per cent protein, but they also ate salads, cooked and raw vegetables, custards and fruit. Meals were divided into two courses, with the first offering a selection of boiled meats, and the second offering roasted or baked meats. During formal feasts or celebrations, each course was preceded by the entrance of a 'subtlety': artworks made from sugar or marzipan, depicting anything from castles, ships and cathedrals to entire battles or hunting scenes.

There were many religious feast days at court. On these occasions, the outer rooms were set up and feasting would carry on well into the night. But during Lent, the 40 days which preceded Easter, it was a different story. Meat was forbidden, with only fish allowed. We follow Cromwell in *Wolf Hall* as he enjoys, or perhaps endures, a Lenten supper at the house of his old friend, Antonio Bonvisi:

It will be the usual tense gathering, everyone cross and hungry: for even a rich Italian with an ingenious kitchen cannot find a hundred ways with smoked eel or salt cod.

After the first meal, Henry often liked to ride out into the royal parklands in search of game, and there are many instances in the series of Cromwell waiting for the king to return from a day in the royal parks or accompanying him on a hunt.

Summer: the king is hunting. If he wants him, he has to chase him, and if he is sent for, he goes.
(Wolf Hall)

Despite the luxuries and proximity to the king, and thus to favour, life at court was expensive. An air of success was crucial to maintain, from a courtier's attire, how much they were willing to lose at the gambling tables, to their retinue and the breed of their horses. The higher you climbed, the more embellished your life became, and for many courtiers, the more debt you accrued. It was also important for young courtiers to be able to demonstrate their prowess: on the tennis court, at the tiltyard and on the hunt. It was Henry VII who revived the cult of chivalry, borrowing from the Burgundian tradition, and was determined to be seen by the rest of Europe as ruling over an opulent, flourishing court. Such themes were at odds with Henry's thrifty nature, but a reputation for magnificence and wealth was equally important to project throughout the new Tudor reign, and he drew from old English myths and legends for inspiration. The royal residences boasted dancing chambers and halls where musicians played while king and court played chess, dice and cards. Archery, tennis and lawn bowls in the expansive gardens were also popular, and both Tudor kings invested in the royal parks, maintaining them and ensuring they were filled with game. Henry VIII was a keen hawker and jouster, holding elaborate tournaments, which were expensive thematic spectacles.

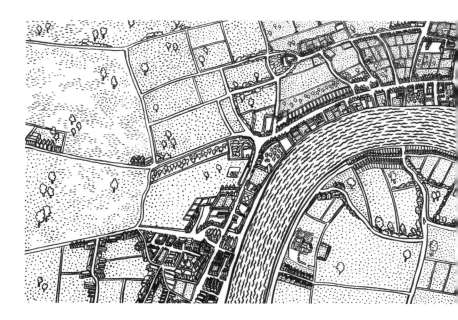

THE ROYAL PALACES

The Tudors were prolific builders, and their numerous estates, from the Tower of London to Nonsuch Palace, served as Tudor fortresses, royal nurseries, royal menageries and symbols of England's wealth. They dominated the Tudor landscape, and even today as we walk the halls of what remains we can catch a glimpse of their lives.

The Tower of London

The Tower of London casts a long shadow over Mantel's series. The huge stone White Tower or castle in the centre of the precinct was built by William of Normandy as a fortress after his invasion in 1066. It was already over 400 years old by the Tudor reign. It was not designed to be a beautiful ornament for the capital, but rather a symbol of Norman might and power. It became a grand royal palace to which various monarchs added surrounding apartments and a defensive wall with watchtowers, and it was used as a royal armoury, treasury, menagerie, and the home of the Royal Mint and the Crown Jewels of England. From the 15th century onwards its

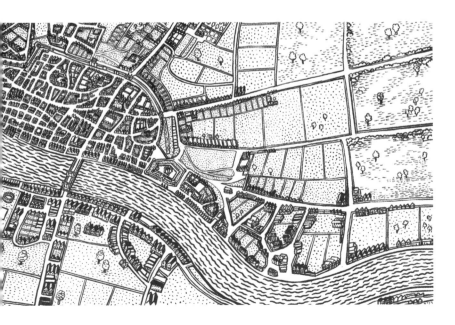

chief role was that of a royal prison although, traditionally, monarchs spent the night in royal lodgings at the Tower prior to their coronation. The Tower would witness countless deaths throughout the centuries, right up until 1941.

Nonsuch Palace

Nonsuch Palace, so called as it was believed no such place could ever exist, was by far the largest of Henry VIII's building projects. It was commissioned in 1538 to mark the birth of his only son and heir, Edward VI, though he

also secretly wanted a palace to rival Francis I's much admired Château de Chambord in the Loire Valley. The reputedly magnificent Nonsuch Palace was unique in that it was an entirely new project, and was built from the ground up to showcase Henry's love of lavish Renaissance architecture. While it remained unfinished even at the time of Henry's death, it was one of the finest buildings of the century, but would unfortunately be dismantled during the reign of Charles II.

HAMPTON COURT

It was Cardinal Wolsey who in 1515 purchased Hampton Court, transforming it from a country estate to a magnificent palace where he could entertain the king and his court. It was the very symbol of Wolsey's artistic tastes and of his wealth, from the majestic state apartments that he built for the king, its lavishly furnished rooms and the hundreds of European tapestries that adorned its many, many walls (and were changed every week) to its beautifully manicured gardens. Ambassadors who were housed there wrote of Hampton Court in the most glowing terms, and his palace was the envy of Europe. Likely inspired by the Bishop of Urbino, Paolo Cortesi, who wrote *De Cardinalatu*, which was more or a less a manual on how to be a cardinal, Wolsey envisioned a palace built in the Renaissance style and spent a decade designing and building an estate unlike any other in England, desired by the king himself who stayed there on several occasions. Wolsey would only enjoy his palace for a few years, gifting it to the king, fully furnished, in 1528, in the hope of saving himself from Henry's wrath.

WINDSOR CASTLE

Built by the Normans in the 11th century, Windsor Castle was one of Henry's most important residences and one the court frequently visited. Originally a fortress, in the 13th century it was transformed into a sumptuous royal palace, and according to *Hall's Chronicle* (1548), Henry VIII spent a great deal of his youth there 'exercising himself daily in shooting, singing, dancing, wrestling, casting of the bar, playing at the recorders, flute, virginals, in setting of songs and making of ballads'. Windsor was also the spiritual home of the Most Noble Order of the Garter, founded by Edward III in 1348, and regarded as the oldest and most prestigious order of chivalry. Henry VIII's grandfather, the Yorkist king Edward IV, had been spurred into competition by the – not quite as ancient, but certainly more glorious – Order of the Golden Fleece, founded by Philip the Good, Duke of Burgundy, in 1430. Under Edward, St George's Chapel at Windsor was redeveloped and the Tudors continued what Edward had begun. It was there that Henry chose to be buried, with his favourite wife Jane Seymour. Although the magnificent tomb he envisaged was never completed, a ledger stone in the Quire marks the site of his burial.

Whitehall

In 1240, Walter de Grey, the Archbishop of York, purchased a beautiful estate in London, and subsequently named it York Place. It was close enough to the Palace of Westminster and could accommodate the royal court, and several monarchs stayed there throughout the centuries.

York Place was rebuilt during the 15th century and Cardinal Wolsey added it to his property portfolio when he was made Archbishop of York. As with Hampton Court, Wolsey expanded and improved the estate to such an extent that it rivalled the royal residences and indeed at one point it had more rooms than the Vatican in Rome. Like a jealous child, Henry loved relieving Wolsey of his most beautiful estates, and took over the magnificent property in 1530, intent on making it one of his main royal residences and to replace Westminster, which was being rebuilt following a devastating fire in 1512. The name was changed from York Place to Whitehall in 1532, a nod to the white stone that had been used to build it.

Placentia

The Palace of Placentia, sometimes simply known as Greenwich, first appears in records in 1417 as an estate given to Humphrey, Duke of Gloucester by his brother, Henry V, which he remodelled and named Bella Court. Upon his death in 1447, the estate was renamed the Palace of Placentia or 'pleasant place' by Henry VI's Queen, Margaret of Anjou, and was brought into the crown's control. Under Henry VII, the palace was revamped and enlarged. It would also be the birthplace of several monarchs, including Henry VIII and his daughters, Mary and Elizabeth. Henry VIII loved the palace so much that it became his primary royal palace, and he celebrated almost every Christmas there.

FAMILIES OF COURT

The old king grew narrow as he aged ... there was no nobleman he did not hold by a debt or bond, and he said frankly that if he could not be loved he would be feared. (*Wolf Hall*)

Today there is a more nuanced view of Tudor politics, that it was less about institutions such as the nobility, Privy Council, the Exchequer and the representation of roles such as Chief Minister and so on, rather it was more to do with the interaction between those institutions and the people, the social networks, clients and patrons, all of which was manifest in the court and its infinite matrix of relationships. Henry's ministers and advisers, including Cromwell, may have wanted to modernize the running of the financial and administrative institutions of the country but, ultimately, they had to bend to the royal will and the king's predilections, and make the best of whatever direction that might take them. The court was a place where, as scholars have noted, 'a name dropped could mean much, and a career could be built through second, third, or fourth-hand access to those in power'. Henry VII rewarded those who fought with him at the Battle of Bosworth, and punished those who chose the wrong side. The nobility also had to contend with a shift in the balance of power: from Henry VII's reign onwards, new men from the ranks of the gentry, the mercantile and the law – those who had little, if any, family fortune or influence but displayed skill, loyalty and ability, those who benefitted from their education and those who brought with them 'a galaxy of talents'.

THE BRANDONS

Originally hailing from the Norfolk coast, the Brandon family emerged from obscurity in the 15th century when William Brandon entered into the service of John de Mowbray, who held the premier dukedom of Norfolk. This connection would propel William's career as he rose in de Mowbray's esteem, with William becoming a senior member of the Duke's council. Throughout the tumultuous years of civil war known as the Wars of the Roses, the Brandons remained loyal Yorkists and were rewarded for their fealty, with William being knighted by Edward IV following the battle of Tewkesbury. However, the loyalty shown to Edward IV wavered during the reign of his brother, Richard III. Richard's reputation was undermined not only by accusations of ruthless ambition, but by the untimely disappearances of his nephews, who had been placed in the Tower of London for their own protection. Family murders for political reasons were not uncommon, but now Richard was suspected of the 'unnatural murder' of his own kin. William's two sons, Thomas and William, took part in a rebellion against the crown, led by Henry Stafford, Duke of Buckingham, later fleeing to Brittany to join the exiled Henry Tudor. In retaliation, King Richard ordered parts of Brandon's lands to be seized. Having fallen out of favour, William quickly left court for the town of Gloucester and remained in self-imposed exile until his death.

His sons, Thomas and William, remained in Brittany with the young Henry Tudor, and were in his army as it sailed from Brittany to England. Of the two Brandon men, only Thomas would survive to see the reign they had fought for – William, who served as standard bearer to Henry Tudor, was slain in battle. But Henry VII would demonstrate throughout his reign his favour to those who had shown him loyalty and dedication during those years of exile, favour which also extended to men's families.

Charles Brandon

William's son, Charles Brandon, grew up in the household of his uncle, Sir Thomas Brandon, and became a leading courtier under Henry VII. By 1507, Brandon himself was serving the king as an esquire of the body. Although he was seven years older than Henry VIII, Charles Brandon was by all accounts his closest companion and friend, and appears in the sources as a larger-than-life figure – as tall as Henry and equally handsome and athletic. Brandon was popular at court, an enthusiastic and skilled jouster, and was one of the few men within Henry's inner circle capable of physically besting the king, although he was careful not to do so too often. On the battlefield Brandon distinguished himself in the sieges of Thérouanne and Tournai in Henry VIII's French campaign of 1513. For his service, he was created Duke of Suffolk.

In *Wolf Hall* Cromwell is less than complimentary of Charles Brandon: '... in his view, Charles Brandon is no brighter than Christopher the mule, though better at fighting and fashion and generally showing off'.

But Mantel's Cromwell forms a good working relationship with Brandon, an element Mantel has drawn from the sources. Brandon could play the buffoon, as we see in Mantel's books, but he was no fool, and was careful not to be a sycophant. He was the ideal companion because he demanded so little of the king. He encouraged Henry's love of physical pursuits and chivalric entertainment – they were very much partners in crime – although this may have been partly calculation. But even Brandon was not exempt from Henry's wrath.

With four marriages throughout his life, Charles Brandon's marital exploits would almost rival his king's. His first marriage, to Margaret Neville, niece to the famed 'kingmaker' Edward Neville, Earl of Warwick, seemed at first a powerful match, but it would end in annulment. His second marriage in 1508 to his former wife's niece, Anne Browne, just a year before Henry came to the throne, was short-lived and ended with her death in 1511. But it was perhaps his third marriage, which brought him a little too close to Henry for comfort, that almost cost him his head.

As one of Henry VIII's trusted friends, Brandon was chosen to participate in the celebrations of the marriage of Henry's younger sister Mary Tudor to the ageing Louis XII, King of France. The marriage was short-lived, with Louis dying weeks after the wedding, and Brandon was dispatched to France to congratulate the new French king, Francis I, but also to negotiate Mary's return to England. According to Brandon, Mary accused him of planning to take her back to England only to have her married off again in a political match against her will and issued him with an ultimatum, that he should marry her now or never marry at all. Brandon, swayed by her tears and his own ambition, risked Henry's wrath and secretly married Mary in Paris, in February 1515.

It was almost entirely down to Wolsey's intervention that Brandon survived Henry's rage, with the two banished from court, the threat of execution looming over Brandon's head. Wolsey interceded for Brandon, but he would still have to repay Mary's marriage portion in annual instalments of £4,000, and she would have to return all the plate and jewels she had taken to France as part of her dowry, as well as the many gifts King Louis had given her. The couple were eventually forgiven and invited back to court, and their marriage would produce four children: Henry, Frances, Eleanor and a second Henry after the death of their first son. But Henry VIII's 'great matter' would place a strain on Henry and his relationship with the couple.

Brandon's dislike of Anne Boleyn and her influence over Henry would intensify, causing friction between Henry and his old friend even after

Brandon's wife, Mary Tudor, died on 25 June 1533, just over three weeks after Anne Boleyn's coronation. Brandon caused further scandal by hastily marrying his 13-year-old ward Catherine Willoughby, originally betrothed to his son, Henry Brandon. The marriage was a cause célèbre at court, with Anne Boleyn especially seeking to promote discord between Brandon and the king, as she was aware that his sympathy was with Katherine. She failed to prise apart their friendship.

Brandon's military career continued as he was appointed as the King's lieutenant in suppressing the rebels of the dangerous rebellion known as the Pilgrimage of Grace in late 1536, and in 1537 he moved to Lincolnshire on the orders of the King. He led the party that met Henry's fourth wife, Anne of Cleves, upon her arrival at Dover in 1540. Within months, he would be involved in the annulment of the marriage, and certainly played some part in Cromwell's spectacular downfall. The last years of Henry VIII's reign were caught up in his desire to recapture some of the glory of his youth in a military triumph over France, and in 1543, Brandon, now almost 60, served as Henry VIII's loyal lieutenant in the North before leading the siege of Boulogne in 1544, in what Henry hoped would be his Agincourt.

Charles Brandon's friendship with Henry VIII remained unbroken throughout his life, which not many men could boast, and when Brandon died unexpectedly on 22 August 1545, Henry VIII sincerely mourned the loss of his brother-in-law and oldest and most loyal friend, arranging for him to be buried in St George's Chapel, Windsor, at his own expense. Brandon was survived by six children, but his two sons, Henry and Charles, died of sweating sickness in July 1551 within hours of each other, and with them the title of the Duke of Suffolk ceased to exist. Brandon's daughters, on the other hand, Anne, Mary, Frances and Eleanor, would marry well and enjoyed powerful positions at court, trajectories that Brandon was able to cultivate from his position close to the crown. He could never have envisioned that his granddaughter, Lady Jane Grey, whose bloodline as the niece of the King of England would bring her into such close proximity to the throne, would also lose her life.

THE PERCYS

The Percys, one of the oldest noble families in England, originating from the village of Percy in Normandy, could date their ancestry to the Norman French William, Duke of Normandy who invaded England in 1066. William de Percy obviously acquitted himself well in battle, as he was rewarded with estates in Yorkshire and Lincolnshire and was awarded a barony. By the

12th century, there was only one female heir, Agnes de Percy, and the direct male line died out, but was revived by her husband, Joscelin de Louvain. Their sons adopted the surname Percy (dropping the French 'de') and their descendants fought for Edward I, Hammer of the Scots, during his battles for dominance over Scotland and Wales, and were granted estates which had once belonged to the Scottish royal family. It was Henry Percy who purchased land in Northumberland, just south of the border with Scotland, which made them formidable as they were the first line of defence against the Scottish. The family also married into the Plantagenet dynasty with the marriage of Henry Percy and Mary of Lancaster, the daughter of Henry Plantagenet, Earl of Lancaster, sometime in 1334. In 1377, his son, unimaginatively called Henry, was created Earl of Northumberland by Richard II.

At this juncture, the Percys literally step out onto the stage. Henry Percy plays a significant role in Shakespeare's *Henry IV*, but he was also the father of another famous Percy – Sir Henry Percy, known as Harry 'Hotspur' – who turned against Richard II in favour of the king's cousin, Henry Bolingbroke, the future Henry IV. Hotspur would go on to raise a rebel army and fight Henry IV as well, at the battle of Shrewsbury in 1403, but was killed before he could inherit the title of Earl of Northumberland. Hotspur's son would redeem the family name, serving Henry V during his wars in France, and upon Henry's death in 1422, Percy was appointed as a member of the council that would govern England during his son Henry VI's minority. The Percy family would have their fair share of family drama and played important roles during the Wars of the Roses, remaining steadfastly loyal to the house of Lancaster. Eventually, the family switched sides, and Henry Percy, 4th Earl of Northumberland, rode at the head of an army to support Richard III's troops, but never actually led them into battle. With Henry VII winning the day at Bosworth, Percy was briefly imprisoned by the new Tudor king, but was later released. He nevertheless went on to meet a violent end, beaten to death in York during a riot.

In Mantel's series, it is his grandson, Henry Percy, heir to the Earldom of Northumberland, who flits in and out of the narrative. Percy served as a page in the household of Cardinal Wolsey, during which time he enjoyed a dalliance with the young Anne Boleyn, but it is not clear how far the relationship went. The Percys were still one of the most powerful families in England, and thus any marriage was a matter of politics. In *Wolf Hall*, an indignant Wolsey hauls the young Percy before him to berate his childishness, before summoning Thomas Boleyn to discuss Anne's conduct.

Thomas is given a dressing down, but as Wolsey notes to Cromwell later:

'They made the rules; they cannot complain if I am the strictest enforcer. Percys above Boleyns.'

Percy was swiftly married to his intended match, Lady Mary Talbot, daughter of the Earl of Shrewsbury. Percy's marriage was a miserable one, but it would come back to haunt Anne in particular just prior to her marriage to Henry, when rumours of the dalliance resurfaced. In *Wolf Hall*, Cromwell and the Boleyns summon Percy to convince him to dispute the rumour. Only Cromwell and Norfolk working together can persuade him to recant.

In *Bring Up the Bodies*, Percy is called upon again by Cromwell, to admit the opposite – a pre-contract with Anne that would make her marriage to Henry invalid. But this time Percy would not be bullied:

'No.' From somewhere, the earl finds a spark of his ancestral spirit, that border fire which burns in the north parts of the kingdom, and roasts any Scot in its path ....
'I cannot help her any more. I can only help myself.'

Percy collapsed after the verdict against Anne in 1536 was read out loud, and never returned to court, dying just over a year later. With no children, he made the King his heir.

The Howards

The Duke of Norfolk fought on the losing side, and his heirs were turned out of their dukedom. They had to work hard, long and hard, to get it back. So, do you wonder, he says, why the Norfolk that is now shakes sometimes, if the king is in a temper? It's because he thinks he will lose all he has, at an angry man's whim.

The Howards had been an integral piece of England's social fabric for centuries. Beginning with William Howard, a lawyer in the county of Norfolk who was summoned to Parliament in 1295, the family sought their elevation through commerce or the law, and married well. When Robert Howard married Margaret Mowbray, daughter of Thomas Mowbray, 1st Duke of Norfolk, he acquired the duchy of Norfolk. Their son, John, eventually succeeded to most of the Mowbray estates and was created Duke of Norfolk and hereditary Earl Marshal in 1483 when the Mowbray line died out. The Howards were a politically powerful family, but they backed the wrong horse (or the wrong rose), with the head of the family, John Howard, killed on the field of Bosworth fighting for Richard III in 1485. During Henry VII's reign, they found themselves in a political eclipse. And worse – for the Howards, being out of favour meant being out of money. John's son, Thomas Howard, would spend his entire career clawing back the Howard reputation. A councillor and military commander for both Henry VII and Henry VIII, he would restore the Howard name, becoming one of the most powerful men at court, enjoying the favour of the Tudor kings. Thomas Howard had at least 16 children across two marriages – to Elizabeth Tilney, and then her cousin, Agnes (for which Howard received a papal dispensation). Many of his children would become powerful members of Henry VIII's court – the young and dashing Edward Howard became Henry VIII's first Lord High Admiral of his navy, but was killed at sea by the French in 1513. Of the other siblings, Edmund Howard would father Catherine, destined to become Henry VIII's fifth queen, and William Howard would serve four Tudor monarchs in various capacities, but it is Thomas Howard, the eldest son, who we know best.

The Duke of Norfolk is, of course, chief of the Howard family and Boleyn's brother-in-law: a sinewy little twitcher, always twitching after his own advantage. (*Wolf Hall*)

Norfolk is almost a comic relief, a tactless, rough bully of a man who, according to Cromwell, lives in the old world of saints, relics and superstition, is convinced Wolsey has sent demons to prick at his heels, and enjoys speaking in vividly violent terms to noble and commoner alike. Historically Norfolk was something of a wolf about court, and he did favour violent turns of phrase, once threatening that he would sooner eat Wolsey alive than allow him to return to favour. His brusque manner was better suited to dealing with the Scots than the easily offended French, and he could be found at court drinking and gambling with various ambassadors, and along with the Duke of Suffolk, he provided the muscular strikes. Following Wolsey's demise, Norfolk became one of the most powerful men at court and resented his niece's influence over the king, even if that influence benefitted his own family. Norfolk was a survivor, extracting himself from Anne Boleyn's fall and presiding over her trial and that of her accused lovers. He also oversaw the execution of his other royal niece, Catherine Howard, and outlived his own son, living to witness the reigns of Edward VI and Mary I.

THE BOLEYNS

Every story needs a villain, and in Mantel's trilogy the Boleyns gratify; history and popular fiction would seem to concur. They, like all the substantial families at court, prospered: they came from yeoman stock, thrived in small businesses, married well in successive generations, and served their king well. But they are not favoured: their success is seen as greed; their marriages into titles and estates is avaricious, their promotions at court only attributable to their promiscuous women. Of all the key players of the Tudor court who orbited the power-rich world created by Henry VIII, the Boleyns – although deftly drawn in Mantel's works – are not necessarily as they appear.

The Boleyns came from modest beginnings in Norfolk, not born into wealth or privilege, but by the 15th century, they were among those who had achieved it. Thomas Boleyn's great-grandfather Geoffrey Boleyn and his wife Alice were one of the great families of Salle, in Norfolk. Their son, also called Geoffrey, launched the family by making a family fortune from trade and commerce. It was this Geoffrey who introduced the Boleyns into the realm of nobility in around 1437 or 1438, marrying Anne Hoo, daughter of Lord Thomas Hoo, a socially superior family to the Boleyns, who offered the all-important connections for the family to advance. He reached the pinnacle of his career when he was elected Lord Mayor of London in 1458. It was Geoffrey who purchased the premier Boleyn estate of Blickling in Norfolk, which is where Geoffrey's son, William, chose to raise his family. William married Margaret Butler, who hailed from Ireland, and whose family held the prestigious title of Earl of Ormond. Thus, their children, including Thomas Boleyn, born in 1477, were raised in a world of wealth and privilege. Thomas, as the eldest son, was well-educated, learned French and Latin and, like generations before him, married well. His wife Elizabeth was the daughter of Thomas Howard, 2nd Duke of Norfolk and Earl of Surrey, one of the most distinguished and powerful families in the country.

Three generations of Boleyns had allied themselves with three powerful and influential families – the Hoos, the Butlers and the Howards. Thomas Boleyn served Henry VII alongside his father William and went on to become one of Henry VIII's leading diplomats; his grandfather, Thomas Butler, was Lord Chamberlain to the first Tudor queen, Elizabeth of York, and then Katherine of Aragon, and his father-in-law, Thomas Howard, Duke of Norfolk, was a powerful and well-respected member of Henry's inner circle. But it was Thomas Boleyn who, through his loyal and dedicated service to the crown, would continue to propel the family to greater fortunes.

Thomas Boleyn

In *Wolf Hall*, Sir Thomas Boleyn 'is the coldest, smoothest man he [Cromwell] has ever seen', but that was a requirement, for he was not only a courtier, but one of the most celebrated, respected and revered ambassadors of Henry's reign, and one of the few to carry out over 15 separate missions. Thomas was a protégé of Cardinal Wolsey and was recommended by Richard Fox, Henry VII's most loyal adviser, confidant and chief architect of his government. Fox and Wolsey handpicked Thomas for his first diplomatic mission in 1512, alongside the most experienced of Henry VII's and Henry VIII's diplomats, and Thomas stood out as a new face in the line-up set by Fox and Wolsey. It is a relationship often overlooked because of Wolsey's subsequent downfall and the role of the 'Boleyn faction' in it. In Mantel's series, Cromwell dislikes having to deal with any of the Boleyns, but historically Cromwell and Thomas Boleyn knew each other as early as 1525, when Boleyn was already a seasoned diplomat and Cromwell new to his post.

While records and correspondence from either Cromwell or Boleyn are scarce, we do know that in 1527, Thomas' sister, Alice, required legal assistance for a matter and wrote to her brother for some recommendations. He immediately put her in touch with Cromwell, and she wrote to him on her brother's recommendation, asking for assistance. Cromwell accepted, and wrote to Thomas in December, informing him that he had agreed to counsel and advise her. Years later, when Anne was queen and Cromwell high in favour, he received a letter from his first cousin, Nicholas Glossop, asking for assistance, and who, by his own admission, was lame, impotent, suffering from gout and blind in one eye. Cromwell quietly sent Glossop to Thomas Boleyn, who took good care of his relative. Glossop later praised Thomas as the man to whom he owed his life.

In Mantel's trilogy, Cromwell shifts from a prominent supporter of the Boleyns to a dangerous adversary. In *Wolf Hall*, Cromwell is scathing of Thomas' rise, but historically his trajectory at court began long before Anne, and cannot be explained simply as a result of a liaison between his daughter and the king. Thomas served in many high-pressure and demanding positions that no mediocre individual would be granted, no matter who currently occupied Henry's bed. These positions included Comptroller of the Household, Treasurer of the Household and Lord Keeper of the Privy Seal, with the last position requiring considerable work and effort. Thomas Boleyn was also a patron of the renowned scholar Desiderius Erasmus, commissioning several important works including *Praeparatio ad mortem*, which focused on how to live one's life in preparation for death.

As the Protestant writer John Strype would write centuries later, 'The world is beholden to this noble peer [Boleyn] for some of the labours that proceeded from the pen of that most learned man [Erasmus].'

Contrary to popular belief, Thomas and his wife did not continue their lives at court following the execution of their children but returned to the peace of Hever Castle. It was Cromwell who continually pressured and bullied Thomas into returning to court. Cromwell replaced Thomas as Lord Privy Seal and, just prior to being admitted to the prestigious order of the Garter in 1537, Cromwell requested that Thomas loan him his best garter badge, a request Thomas was forced to comply with. As a member, Thomas should have been present for Cromwell's admission, but he is conspicuously absent; the letter he sent to Cromwell with the badge made it clear that Thomas did not voluntarily give his collar to Cromwell and he would not leave Hever for the ceremony. It is also worth noting that Cromwell was particularly harsh on Thomas when it came to payment of legal subsidies and rents, insisting that all of Thomas' payments be paid strictly on time, though he never pressured any other nobles, including Norfolk, all of whom were in arrears. Thomas Boleyn and his brother-in-law, Thomas Howard, would henceforth have a fractious relationship. In July of 1537, Norfolk complained to Cromwell that Thomas' minstrel had sung derogatory songs about him and he was certain that Thomas had approved of it. Cromwell urged Thomas to punish the minstrel, but it seems that Thomas ignored him. Historically, Thomas had little interest in the machinations of court, and would rather have been left alone in the comfort of Hever Castle, where he cared for his aging mother, but Henry and Cromwell had other ideas.

George Boleyn

George Boleyn is commonly seen as a handsome but useless ornament of the court. Promiscuous, wild, cruel and arrogant, Mantel's version insults Cromwell, belittles his wife, Jane, and smirks behind his hand at Henry. But there is more to George historically. George's career blossomed during Anne's rise, but he struggled to be seen as a man of skill and determination, with every mark of favour attributed to his sister. He was used as an almost glorified messenger between England and France, never assigned to a proper diplomatic mission, though he was more than capable. He was close to his sister and ultimately became a central member of the colourful circle of courtiers that surrounded her. The pair were similar in temperament, sharing the same intellectual and aesthetic interests and developing a passion for the New Learning of Renaissance humanism, with

George dedicating translations of devotional texts to his sister. Surprisingly, George was a man capable of deep spirituality. George haunts Cromwell in *The Mirror And The Light*, as we flash back to Cromwell visiting George in the Tower, where for the first time George is not depicted as a buffoon, but an innocent man who understands why he is to be destroyed. Historically George was concerned for those to whom he owed money and those who depended on his patronage and it is only in the third instalment that Mantel inches towards a more historical and realistic portrayal. Unfortunately for George, the false charges of incest and cruelty to his wife have found their way into fiction, and back again into history. We nevertheless are left with one poignant last offering from George Boleyn – a falcon in Beauchamp Tower, which George likely carved. It is not just his sister's crest of the white falcon, it is his father's falcon, the Butler Falcon, a sorrowful, melancholic, moving tribute to his family to whom he had been so dedicated.

Mary Boleyn

Mary Boleyn is a kind little blonde, who is said to have been passed all around the French court before coming home to this one.
(*Wolf Hall*)

Historically, Mary Boleyn is somewhat elusive in the sources, but in fiction she has a voice, and seems to be a popular narrator. In Mantel's books she is sweet, lively, but calculating, enticing Cromwell into some degree of intimacy, which Cromwell later believes is because she is pregnant, though nothing comes of the rumour. There is no love lost between Mantel's Mary and her siblings, with Anne often her tormentor in the series, but we have no real indication as to how close they were. Like her sister, Mary served Princess Mary Tudor at the French court, and it was rumoured that she was also mistress to the libertine French king, Francis I, though this has never been proven. Upon her return to the English court, she became Henry VIII's mistress, and there is some uncertainty as to whether her two children, Henry and Catherine, had royal blood. Mary first married William Carey, who came from a well-connected family, in 1520. As a mark of respect to the Boleyn family, Henry allowed them to wed in the royal chapel at Greenwich palace, and there is evidence that Thomas Boleyn tried to mentor his son-in-law in the politics of court. Carey died of the sweating sickness in 1528, the same outbreak that decimated the country and Cromwell's own household. In *Wolf Hall*, Mary Boleyn is quickly on the prowl for another husband, and surprisingly indiscreet in her conversations with Cromwell regarding her sister, Anne:

She is selling herself by the inch ... She wants a present in cash for every advance above her knee.

We have no evidence that Cromwell had any relationship with Mary whatsoever, just a letter written to Cromwell following her banishment from court for marrying the wrong man. In 1534, Mary secretly married William Stafford, a soldier with few prospects. For the sister of the Queen, it exposed the Boleyn family to ridicule. Writing to Cromwell, she begged for his assistance, though it is not clear that he lifted a finger in her defence. The Mary Boleyn of *Wolf Hall* would have had better luck, with Cromwell deciding to bring in Thomas Boleyn:

He will humiliate him – in his genial fashion – and make him give Mary an annuity.

Thomas would give Mary an annual pension of £100, as he did for his daughter-in-law, Jane. But prior to his death, Thomas had begun to reconcile with his only living daughter, and an indenture between the King and Mary and William Stafford shows that Mary would receive a number of her family's estates. Thomas had clearly negotiated with Cromwell and the King before his death and left his younger brother James and his lawyer to ensure it was carried out – Thomas may have had a fractious relationship with his daughter but the evidence shows us that he would not have wanted her to go through the rest of her life destitute. Mary would only survive her parents by four years, but her children, Henry and Catherine, would go on to live successful lives at the court of their cousin, Elizabeth I.

2
CROMWELL
ASCENDS

THE CARDINAL'S MAN

Thomas Cromwell is now a little over 40 years old. He is a man of strong build, although not tall. Various expressions pass across his face, and only one is readable: a look of stifled amusement. His hair is dark, heavy and waving, and his small eyes, which are very sharp, light up in conversation, so the Spanish ambassador will tell us shortly. His speech is low and rapid, his manner assured; he is at home in courtroom or waterfront, bishop's palace or inn yard. He can draft a contract, train a falcon, draw a map, stop a street fight, furnish a house and fix a jury. He knows new poetry, and can recite it in Italian. He works all hours, first up and last to bed. He makes money and he spends it. He will take a bet on anything.

Cromwell had made an extremely favourable impression on Wolsey following his dismantling of various monasteries, and from 1524 we can place him in Wolsey's household, being referred to as one of the Cardinal's counsel – a highly sought-after position. But interestingly, Cromwell was not working in the public sector for the Cardinal, but rather he dealt with Wolsey's private matters just as he had done for the Greys. When we first meet the adult Cromwell in *Wolf Hall*, he has just arrived from York following two weeks away on Wolsey's business, and we are given a glimpse of his life in service to the Cardinal:

He's been to his clerks at Gray's Inn and borrowed a change of linen. He's been east to the city, to hear what ships have come in and to check the whereabouts of an off-the-books consignment he is expecting.

Cromwell's life would have been a whirlwind of errands, negotiations and transactions on behalf of his master, Wolsey, all of which Cromwell ran concurrently with his private legal work, commissioned from clients from the Cardinal's network, who came to him with their problems. As the Cardinal's man, Cromwell was also well placed to appraise the usefulness or otherwise of those who sought the Cardinal's patronage; the extant letters are hopeful and flattering, addressed to the 'right worshipful Mr. Cromwell', begging the Cardinal's favour. Wolsey relied heavily on Cromwell to manage his ambitious programme to amalgamate various crumbling and neglected monasteries and divert the proceeds to fund Wolsey's college, as Mantel has Cromwell say, to convert property into gold. This task was far more complex than Wolsey had ever envisioned, and Cromwell's masterful execution of the assignment is a testament to his organizational acumen.

Cromwell was hands on, supervising the surveyance of property and overseeing transfers and various settlements of the clergy and nuns who ran the monasteries, as well as dealing with travellers, the poor and the sick, and converting these properties into funds. Cromwell usually oversaw every stage personally and frequently came up against protest and obstruction; in these cases he was instructed by Wolsey to use money to make the problem go away.

His skill with property was as useful as his skill with languages; in *Wolf Hall*, Wolsey asks if he has any Spanish, as he feels that it might be more useful to have friends in the queen's household. With the king's growing misgivings about his first marriage to Katherine of Aragon, sometime between 1526 and 1527, Mantel's Wolsey is talking about spies who might report back on what the queen said in unguarded moments thinking she would not be overheard or understood when she heard the news that the king wished to marry another woman.

As Wolsey notes, this is not Henry's problem or Katherine's problem – it is the Cardinal's.

KATHERINE OF ARAGON

In *Wolf Hall* we are told Cromwell admires Katherine. Outwardly she wears the clothes of a queen, 'gowns so bristling with gemstones that they look as if they are designed less for beauty than to withstand blows from a sword'; however, underneath 'she wears the habit of a Franciscan nun'.

Katherine of Aragon had more royal blood than Henry and all his wives put together, a far superior royal education, and more royal dignity. Born during a military campaign, she was a woman whose military knowledge was equal to that of any prince of Europe. A woman who loved, lost, and never wavered in her determination that Henry could not dismantle her life on a whim. Perceptions of Henry's first queen are often coloured by what became known as the king's 'great matter', but there is more to Katherine than the divorce, she is more than an unhappy element in a love triangle.

Katherine was born into one of the most powerful families of Europe, the daughter of Isabella of Castile and Ferdinand of Aragon, both monarchs in their own right, who founded an impressive dynastic power. She grew up in the sophisticated, unrivalled majesty of the Alhambra, the palace fortress complex in Granada, Spain, her parents ensuring she and her sisters received the same education as their brother, Juan. Under her tutor

Alessandro Geraldini, Katherine studied arithmetic, canon and civil law, classical literature, genealogy and heraldry, history, philosophy, religion, theology and languages such as Spanish, Latin, French and Greek. She was a highly desirable catch, just what the Tudors needed. The match raised some eyebrows, as the Spanish ambassador at the Tudor court, Rodrigo de Puebla, remarked: 'Bearing in mind what happens every day to the kings of England, it is surprising that Ferdinand and Isabella should dare think of giving their daughter at all.'

Katherine had a legitimate and stronger claim to the English throne than King Henry VII. She was the great-great-grand-daughter of the second wife of John of Gaunt, Constance of Castile. In contrast, Henry VII was a descendant of Gaunt's third marriage to Katherine Swynford, whose children were all illegitimate. The advantageous alliance of Katherine and Prince Arthur, who represented the union of the houses of Lancaster and York, now further validated the House of Tudor, gaining the acceptance of European monarchs and the Pope, and their claim to the English throne. The match was approved and they were married by proxy on 19 May 1499.

THE SPANISH PRINCESS

Katherine arrived in England in 1501, and Henry VII immediately wished to view England's prize. Growing impatient with her slow progress from the coast, in an impetuous gesture he rides down to meet the Spanish party. In *Wolf Hall*, Wolsey describes King Henry striding into the rooms where Katherine was staying, where upon seeing her for the first time he is rendered speechless. Katherine was a beautiful, 16-year-old princess and her marriage to the 15-year-old Prince Arthur excited the entire country, with its promise of prosperity, unity with the great kingdom of Spain, and a long succession of progeny. Katherine and Arthur were wed, moving first to Baynard's Castle, then Windsor, and finally to Ludlow in Wales, where the young couple would set up royal residence. Tragically, within a year, Arthur was dead, and Katherine quickly made it known that the marriage had never been consummated. Whether this declaration was calculated, or whether she was telling the truth, we shall never know. In *Wolf Hall*, Cromwell contemplates a young, widowed Katherine he never knew, who insisted she was still a virgin. Perhaps they should have verified her statement at the time, he thinks – Katherine, although fearful, would not have objected:

'But they never asked her to prove what she claimed; perhaps people were not so shameless in those days.'

Only six years older than the young Prince Henry, Katherine still possessed all the qualities found in an ideal queen, but it seemed that both Henry and his father, the recently widowed Henry VII, had their eye on her. Thankfully, Katherine's parents rejected the proposal of the elder king and it was agreed that Prince Henry would wed his brother's widow.

The decision to betroth her to Arthur's brother, Henry, rescued both dowry and alliance, and pleased both sets of parents. But there was an issue: the marriage between Katherine and Arthur had created an affinity between Katherine and Henry. The devout Ferdinand requested a papal dispensation, and accordingly a papal bull was granted by Julius II on 26 December 1503, which allowed the marriage to proceed. However, a key enjoinder in the bull was a single, potent word, *forsitan*, meaning 'perhaps'; perhaps Katherine and Arthur consummated their marriage, but perhaps they had not.

Decades later in *Wolf Hall*, when looking for a pretext on which to annul the king's first marriage, Cromwell notes that the language used in the bull was carefully chosen to cover either eventuality, and that the answer to his problem was more likely to be found in the Spanish documents relating to the marriage, 'not squabbling in a court of law over a shred of skin and a splash of blood on a linen sheet'.

Cromwell first hears of Henry's marital doubts while sitting in Wolsey's chambers; it is 1527. Wolsey ponders how he might find Henry a son to rule after him. Cromwell replies 'If you cannot find him a son ... you must find him a piece of scripture. To ease his mind.' They reject Deuteronomy, which advises that a man should marry the wife of a dead brother, on the basis that the king 'doesn't like Deuteronomy'. Instead, Henry thinks he might appeal to Pope Clement VII to release him from 'sin' by ending the marriage, as popes had done for other European royalty, and had selected the pertinent passage in Leviticus 20:21, which forbids a man to marry his brother's widow or else they would be childless. Wolsey explains that the king interprets 'childless' as having no sons.

THE RIVALS AND HENRY'S 'GREAT MATTER'

Despite almost 20 years of marriage, Henry was determined to be rid of Katherine. When she finally was apprised of the situation, of course she was outraged and suspected that Wolsey was behind the plot; historically Wolsey and Katherine had a slightly tense relationship. Queen Katherine had been brought up in a household where her parents were monarchs who governed jointly, her rightful place at least should be sole advisor to the king. She was mistrustful of Wolsey's desire to be the king's confidant; and his partiality towards the French, the traditional enemies of the Spanish Empire, made her deeply suspicious.

When Katherine was confronted by Henry and his advisers about the validity of their marriage, without hesitation she assured them that it was valid because she and the 'sickly' 15-year-old Arthur had never consummated their union. She was a virgin when she married Henry; there was no sex, no affinity, no impediment. What Katherine hadn't grasped, perhaps blinded by her faith and love for her husband, was that her virginity wasn't the point, it was merely a weapon. At first it seemed simple, one pope had allowed the marriage, so another pope could disallow it, or so Wolsey and Henry might have thought, but it soon became very clear that Katherine had a powerful ally, her nephew, the Holy Roman Emperor Charles V, a monarch that not even the Pope was willing to offend. The Pope would never accede to this request, therefore, it was more prudent and propitious to ask for the case be heard in England where the outcome could be controlled. Pope Clement VII agreed to this and appointed a commission, consisting of Cardinal Wolsey and another legate, Cardinal Campeggio, to hear the case, while the decision of the commission was still to be referred to Rome for confirmation.

Mantel's Cromwell was there to witness it all. The court is a secret one, and is likely to rule in Henry's favour, but Wolsey is not confident this will be enough, 'he does not know ... what the legatine court can do for him, beyond this preparatory step; since Katherine, surely, is bound to appeal to Rome.' Which she would certainly do. However, before a formal trial could commence, word was received that the troops of Katherine's nephew, Charles V, had sacked Rome and taken the Pope captive.

Charles may not have given the order, but it was done in his name, and now this young, ambitious ruler held half of Europe as well as the papacy in his hands. On 8 December 1528, Cardinal Campeggio arrived in London, sent by the Pope to stall proceedings. In the interim, Katherine managed to produce Pope Julius II's original dispensation, which had allowed her to marry Henry, alarming Wolsey. Both Wolsey and Campeggio had hoped Katherine, whose destiny had been the throne of England since she had been betrothed to Arthur since the age of three, would simply flee to a convent, an offer which she refused. Katherine appealed to Rome, to her nephew, and to anyone else who would listen. Formal proceedings finally began on 31 May 1529 in the Legatine Court at Blackfriars, London. On 21 June, Katherine herself was called.

In *Wolf Hall* Mantel steps away from one of the most famous speeches of the period, in which Katherine knelt at her husband's feet and pleaded her case:

I have been to you a true, humble and obedient wife, ever comfortable to your will and pleasure, that never said or did any thing to the contrary thereof, being always well pleased and contented with all things wherein you had any delight or dalliance, whether it were in little or much. I never grudged in word or countenance, or showed a visage or spark of discontent. I loved all those whom ye loved, only for your sake, whether I had cause or no, and whether they were my friends or enemies. This twenty years or more I have been your true wife and by me ye have had divers children, although it hath pleased God to call them out of this world, which hath been no default in me. And when ye had me at first, I take God to my judge, I was a true maid, without touch of man. And whether it be true or no, I put it to your conscience.

Katherine is as formidable in fiction as she was historically, and there is a sense that the real Cromwell had a deep respect for her strength and determination. Mantel's Cromwell is equally admiring, her speech 'resounds from here to Paris, from here to Madrid, to Rome. She is standing on her status, she is standing on her rights; the windows are rattled, from here to Constantinople. What a woman she is, he remarks in Spanish.'

Clement procrastinated for as long as possible, despite the constant pressure from Wolsey, who felt, rightly, that his very life depended on the right outcome.

In July 1529 Campeggio adjourned the hearing until October, as this was the time for the harvest in Rome and its environs, and this allowed the Legatine Court a summer recess. But the court would never sit again, for news soon reached England that Pope Clement had approved Katherine's appeal and recalled the case to Rome. This was the end for Wolsey. Cromwell considers the news:

That evening with Wolsey he believes, for the first time, that the cardinal will come down. If he falls, he thinks, I come down with him.
(*Wolf Hall*)

Wolsey had always been deeply unpopular with the nobility, who envied his ability and the king's reliance on him, but he had done nothing to remedy it or win over his enemies. But without Henry's favour, Wolsey was vulnerable. Within months of the legatine recess, Wolsey presided over the meetings of the king's council, but unbeknownst to him, charges were being drawn up against him. As Mantel's Cromwell tells us, 'he is charged with asserting a foreign jurisdiction in the king's realm ... with exercising his role as papal legate ... he has always been, more imperious than the king. For that, if it is a crime, he is guilty.'

In a scene near the beginning of *Wolf Hall*, and the first scene in the BBC production: the great dukes of Norfolk and Suffolk march into York Place and demand the Great Seal from Wolsey, as Cromwell, in rapid undertones, advises his master. There was no time even to protest: on 9 October 1529, Wolsey was indicted in the Court of the King's Bench under praemunire, a lesser form of treason. On 17 October, he surrendered the great seal and formally resigned as Lord Chancellor. He was allowed to leave London and make his way north to his diocese of York.

ENTRY TO COURT

With Wolsey's fall, men like Cromwell, Stephen Vaughan and George Cavendish feared they would share their master's fate. Cavendish even recounts a weeping Cromwell lamenting that he would likely lose everything he had worked for, a scene which Mantel includes, though her Cromwell is weeping for his daughters. He had worked with Wolsey for years and he alone knew all of Wolsey's private as well as public affairs; he was allowed to conclude Wolsey's outstanding matters, often attending court on Wolsey's behalf, and also took charge of his estates and household goods.

In *Wolf Hall*, Cromwell is determined to intervene on his master's behalf, to convince Henry, and more importantly, Anne Boleyn and her allies, that Wolsey is the best bet for achieving their goal of an annulment. Following Wolsey's fall, he approaches the king as he prepares for a day of hunting, but this is not, as Henry reminds Cromwell, the first time they have met. Seven years prior, in 1523, Cromwell had entered Parliament and obtained a seat in the House of Commons – though he would not maintain his seat for long, he must have made an impression. His speech still survives, in which he eloquently raised issues over Henry's proposed war with France, objecting to the request to the House from Wolsey for more money to fund such a campaign. It was rather daring for Cromwell to oppose his patron at the time, and attempt to reason with a young king who dreamed of conquering France. We do not know if Henry ever reproached him for the speech, but in *Wolf Hall*, Mantel imagines what it might look like: here is Henry berating Cromwell for dismissing Henry's earlier capture of the French town of Thérouanne:

'So what do you want? You want a king who doesn't fight? You want me to huddle indoors like a sick girl?'
'That would be ideal, for fiscal purposes.'

Following this meeting, Wolsey receives cartloads of furnishings for Esher Palace, which gives Cromwell hope that Henry missed his former Chancellor. We also know that Cromwell made his mark, with his friend, John Russell, writing to him following the meeting with Henry to tell him how well he had impressed the king.

ANNE BOLEYN

In *Wolf Hall*, even Anne Boleyn remarks on Henry's growing admiration for his new man, Cromwell:

'Alors,' Anne says softly, 'suddenly, everything is about you. The king does not cease to quote Master Cromwell.' She pronounces it as if she can't manage the English: Cremuel.

We do not know when Cromwell first met Anne Boleyn in person, but Mantel has imagined it thus: it is Lent, 1529 and as Henry is spending time with Katherine 'for the sake of appearances', Anne sends for Cromwell 'to see if he offers any amusement'.

Anne Boleyn may well be one of the most famous and enigmatic women in English history; although so many have pronounced their like or dislike for her, there is so much about her life that eludes us. Evidence suggests Anne was born at Blickling, Norfolk, anywhere between 1500 and 1509 to Thomas and Elizabeth Boleyn, though it is debatable whether she was the elder or younger daughter (Mantel has favoured the latter). Her grandfather, Thomas Howard, and great grandfather, Thomas Butler, were two of the most influential men in the country. During her childhood, her father, Thomas, was favoured and mentored by one of the most powerful women in Europe, Margaret of Austria, the aunt of the future Charles V.

Thomas was ambitious for all his children and saw that they had a good education, but by securing her a place at Margaret's court in Mechelen, one of the most sophisticated courts in Europe, he opened up extraordinary opportunities for his daughter. In 1514, Thomas had further secured a position for Anne at the French court to serve Henry VIII's sister, Mary, who had married the ageing French king, Louis XII. On 1 January 1515, Louis died, perhaps not unexpectedly, for Thomas very quickly secured Anne a position in the household of Louis' daughter, the new French queen, Claude, wife of the recently anointed King Francis I. Anne spent seven years in France, and was able to see her father often during his many French embassies. She returned to England sometime in 1521–22, with a European education

and decidedly French sense
of sophistication, which
immediately set her apart
from her English counterparts. Her intelligence,
charm and wit were very much her father's traits, as was her talent for
French. She took part in a court masque at Cardinal Wolsey's residence
at Whitehall; her role was Perseverance, which is related to Fortitude, one
of the Four Cardinal virtues, but a strikingly apt role for Anne.

We have numerous portraits of Anne, all depicting a very different
woman. Hers was a tall stature, with a slender neck and dark auburn hair and
eyes, described as 'black and beautiful'.

Mantel has reimagined Anne Boleyn, which has caused considerable
controversy. Mantel's Anne is a calculating being, with a 'cold slick brain' at
work. Her eyes are not beautiful – 'they are hungry'. Throughout the series,
Cromwell never warms to Anne; he thinks he understands her, but then she
seems to confuse him. There is distrust and distance between them. The real
Anne is difficult to fathom – she was said to be tempestuous, intelligent,
politically astute, beguiling and rash, but she was also generous, devout
and loyal, and it is hard not to empathize with her. We have reinvented her
over the centuries, and still continue to discover the real Anne, but Mantel
has enhanced her more negative traits. Of course, Anne enters Cromwell's
life in *Wolf Hall* at a time when his beloved master is suffering banishment,
humiliation and the destruction of his entire career, and Anne is one of
the provocateurs: Cromwell, though he might not admit it, cannot be
dispassionate about the downfall of his great friend, Wolsey. It was for all
to see, Henry's passionate yet irrational pursuit of Anne, his intent to woo
her while still married. Unsurprisingly, she rejected his advances, he would
have to marry her if he wanted to have her. In the series, Cromwell sees only
calculation, Anne selling herself by the inch, but the real Anne had every
right to demand more from Henry – she was the daughter of a well-respected
man of court, she came from a good family, she was worth something. The
fictional Anne captures the feeling perfectly: 'I was always desired. But now
I am valued. And that is a different thing, I find.'

TUDOR
PASTIMES

FEAST DAYS AND HOLY DAYS

Henry's matrimonial drama captivated the country – Henry had a queen, and a queen-in-waiting, and what must have felt like two rival courts. For the sake of appearances, Henry returned to his wife for important holidays, lest foreign eyes viewed his desire to divorce Katherine as anything other than a matter of conscience. Tudor lives were marked by holy days, saints' days and feasts – in particular Christmas, Lady Day (25 March), Midsummer Day (24 June), Michaelmas (29 September) and Hallowtide. In the series, Mantel marks her story with these events, as they marked their calendars, and they serve as signposts, guiding us through each year.

HALLOWTIDE

Hallowtide consisted of three feast days: All Hallows' Eve on 31 October; All Hallows' Day on 1 November; and All Souls' Day on 2 November. It was believed to be the time when the physical and supernatural worlds were at their closest, and people would pray for the souls of their departed loved ones, attempting to shorten their time in purgatory. Soul cakes were baked by the wealthy on All Hallows' Eve and were left with glasses of wine, ale or milk for spirits to enjoy. On All Souls' Day, soul cakes were given to the poor, mainly children, who went 'souling' where they begged door-to-door for treats. In return for these treats, children would pray for the souls of the dead.

The year Cromwell's wife and daughters die of the sweating sickness, Mantel's Cromwell keeps vigil for the dead at Wolsey's beloved Esher Palace, sitting awake, haunted by family members just beyond his reach. And the Hallowtide season again causes him to reflect that his loved ones are *dead to the autumn aroma of pine resin and apple candles, of soul cakes baking*. It is a time of reflection, as the barrier between this world and the next weakens, and Mantel's Cromwell feels the faint touches of his daughter's hands on the pages of his book.

TUDOR CHRISTMAS

While our modern Christmas celebration is heavily influenced by the Victorian traditions, we do still retain some traditions that the Tudors would have recognized. It began with Advent, a time of fasting, which lasted four weeks prior to Christmas. In *Wolf Hall* Cromwell prepares for the feast, storing expensive ingredients that hint at the wealth found within his household:

Advent: first the fast and then the feast. In the store rooms, raisins, almonds, nutmegs, mace, cloves, liquorice, figs and ginger.

Christmas Eve was the last night of fasting – traditionally, families brought home large logs, which were then decorated with ribbons and placed upon the hearth, burning throughout the 12 days of Christmas.

Christmas Day began before dawn with Mass, with each member of the congregation holding a lit taper. More masses would be held a little later in the day. In preparation for the highly anticipated feast to come, plum porridge would be served, thought to line the stomach prior to the main meal of the day. Not to be confused with its later incarnation as a plum pudding, this was a thick broth of mutton or beef, which was boiled along with plums, spices, dried fruits, breadcrumbs and wine. Then, finally, the country broke its fast with the Christmas feast, which heralded the 12 days of Christmas. The Tudor court became a scene of chaotic mirth and opulence, with over 1,000 people dining at the court. For Christmas dinner, almost every household would have enjoyed the seasonal favourite – brawn – a dish made from the head of a cow or pig. For wealthy households, and certainly at court, the feasts were not just about the food, but an extravagant display of wealth and ingenuity. The first course was traditionally a boar's head, which had been stuffed with mince, smeared with mustard and dressed in rosemary, bay leaves and various exotic spices. An apple was placed in its mouth and it was carried into the Great Hall on a great platter by the Steward of the Household. This was only the beginning. It might take less time to list the meats which did not adorn the great tables of the court, but among other dishes, the king and his court would have feasted on swan, peacock, goose, pheasant and an assortment of game birds and fowl. Turkeys were introduced during Henry's reign, and he was one of the first kings to include it as part of the Christmas feast. The Tudor Christmas pie was also a spectacle. A carnivore's delight, the contents consisted of a turkey, stuffed with a goose, stuffed with a chicken, stuffed with a partridge and then stuffed with a pigeon. These were sealed within a pastry case called a coffin, and served alongside hare, and any other birds that had not made it into the main pastry case.

Not that Christmas was simply about eating. The 12 days of revelry were punctuated by a host of festive activities, from pageants to masques, all presided over by the Lord of Misrule, rather than the king, who also had to obey the temporary Lord throughout the festivities. 'Boy bishops', chorister boys chosen from cathedral choirs, took the place of adult prelates and were allowed the same privileges as Lords of Misrule. Appointed on St Nicholas Day, 6 December, they 'held office' until 28 or 29 December; they were treated as if they were actual bishops, enjoyed real episcopal power and took all the services the adult bishop would have taken, with Mass being the only exception.

Throughout the series, Cromwell experiences very different Christmases. Before the death of his wife and daughters, he remembers making his daughter Grace a set of wings for the nativity play, but rather than the usual goose feathers, he makes them out of peacock feathers. It is also at Christmastide when Anne Boleyn first appears at court, dancing during the Christmas feast, in a yellow dress. Moving forwards through the years of *Wolf Hall*, Cromwell is summoned just after Christmas, at a time when it was believed that again the walls between this world and the afterlife thinned, and the dead walked among the living. Henry tells of a dream in which he saw his dead brother, Prince Arthur:

He looked sad, so sad. He seemed to say I stood in his place. He seemed to say, you have taken my kingdom, and you have used my wife. He has come back to make me ashamed.

We also see Cromwell's household coming together for their own festivities throughout the 1530s as Cromwell's position at court strengthens. It was the custom to exchange gifts at New Year, and for the court these presents could be deeply political. In *Wolf Hall*, Henry rather greedily questions Chapuys, the Imperial ambassador, about the offerings he may receive from the Emperor, adding 'The French have already made me great gifts.'

The Feast of the Epiphany on 6 January marked the end of the processions, feasts and festivities, but the Yuletide season officially ended on 2 February, with the solemn celebration of Candlemas, the feast of the Purification of the Virgin Mary. Every church would be aglow with hundreds of candles when the king and queen made their procession to Mass. A new year had begun, but it was anyone's guess during Henry's reign who would live to see it out.

THE TRAPPINGS OF A GENTLEMAN

Sport and pastimes in Tudor England evolved depending on the preferences of each monarch. Henry VII was fond of hunting throughout his life, and despite his deteriorating eyesight in his later years, he continued to indulge in the sport. Henry VIII, however, excelled at everything in his youth. The court bubbled with entertainment – gambling, playing shuffleboard and tennis in Henry's palaces and, in good weather, hunting, hawking, archery contests and racing greyhounds. But sport and leisure were controlled by the government, dictating crucial aspects according to one's rank and ensuring a distance between commoners and the nobility. Henry VIII passed a law in 1512 which banned commoners from indulging in leisurely pursuits such as tennis, cards, dice, bowls and skittles. Only during the Christmas season were these laws relaxed, but there were still certain activities, such as jousting and hunting, that belonged solely to the higher echelons of society.

HUNTING

Like jousting, one had to be of a certain rank or status to be able to participate in the hunt. And, like jousting, it was believed that hunting kept one physically and mentally fit in preparation for war, should one arise. The royal hunt was quite the spectacle, with the nobles of the court, including women, riding out on horseback with their respective dogs – spaniels, buckhounds or greyhounds. Certain breeds were used to track the animal, while others would be used to bring it down. Even the dogs one owned were a symbol of status or position and a matter of pride – the wrong size or colour could expose one to mockery, which Gregory Cromwell tries to explain to his father in *Wolf Hall*. His black greyhounds are a source of amusement, 'They say, why would you have dogs that people can't see at night? Only felons have dogs like that.'

The hunt commenced with loud trills of the Huntmaster's whistle, which would send the dogs tearing into the forest followed by their owners. Henry could spend the whole day in the saddle; the duration of the hunt dependent on whether he brought his prey to the ground. There were numerous royal parks attached to the various palaces that were ideal for hunting, but when the court was in progress, Henry often stayed in hunting lodges or with his hosts, members of the nobility, who had to ensure their own lands were suitably well stocked.

Henry VIII loved to hunt with his companions, but several of his queens often participated too. Throughout Henry's courtship of Anne she often

accompanied him, also taking pleasure in the sport. Even in a letter written by Henry to Anne in the early days of their affair, he boasted of a stag he had hunted: 'And to cause you yet oftener to remember me, I send you, by the bearer of this, a buck killed late last night by my own hand, hoping that when you eat of it you may think of the hunter.' But in *Wolf Hall* Cromwell observes: 'You do not know where the chase will end, or when.'

HAWKING

Hawking or falconry, the hunting of small wild game or birds using highly trained birds of prey, had existed for centuries in Europe and Asia, and was something of a sport as well as an art form. It was one of the most popular sports of the aristocracy, among women and men alike, with Henry VIII rearing flocks of birds such as pheasant specifically for the sport. Unlike jousting or hunting, commoners could own birds of prey, but the strict hierarchy attached to it, namely the type of bird you could own, demonstrated your status. Kings and emperors would use rarer birds such as eagles, gyrfalcons or merlins; dukes could own merlins or goshawks; earls were allowed to own peregrine falcons; and commoners could only use sparrowhawks. Courtiers paid a hefty price if they owned a bird above their station. Hawking was expensive – the birds had to be trained and then housed in mews, but it was all part of the display; even the quality of the equipment used by Henry and his nobles was a testament to their wealth and taste. Henry owned a range of hawking paraphernalia, including hawk's hoods studded with jewels, gold and silver whistles used to direct the birds, and velvet gauntlets on which they would perch. Throughout the series, Henry is often hawking, and as the books progress, it is Cromwell who joins him, a subtle display of his growing influence and position within the court.

JOUSTING

Jousting was, without doubt, the most exclusive and prestigious activity throughout England and Europe in the 16th century. It was a favourite of Henry VIII, who had not been allowed to participate in his youth as the only surviving male heir, but with good reason. For all its glamour and spectacle, it was not for show, but rather an intensely physically demanding sport, requiring strength, a high level of fitness, agility and prowess. Participants not only had to stay upright on their horse attired in heavy armour, they also had to balance, aim the lance and charge, bracing for the inevitable contact, which might result in the opponent's lance splintering into the body, face or worse. Henry and the young men of court often participated, but even the older generation, men like Thomas Boleyn and the Duke of Norfolk, took part.

Jousting became a highly formalized and detailed event, which required a great deal of planning. Two challengers were placed at either end of a rectangular area known as the 'list', with a 'tilt', a wooden barrier running down the middle of the area that designated their side. This was an opportunity not only to show off one's athletic skills, but for the monarchs and their court to show their wealth and power. From the specially built stands draped with royal and noble heraldry to the decorations and attire of the court, the theme of chivalry and majesty was projected on a public stage, not just for the commoners to enjoy, but also for foreign dignitaries and ambassadors, who reported to their masters all the splendour they witnessed.

The aim of the joust was to strike one's opponent on specific parts of their armour or their shield. Failing that, they would also attempt to unseat their opponent. Points were awarded depending on where a blow was struck or if either opponent broke their lance on the other. These lances were not sharpened, but they were still dangerous enough to cause serious damage. In *Bring Up the Bodies*, Cromwell notes the points awarded did not represent the true cost of the sport:

A touch on the breastplate is recorded, but not fractured ribs. A touch on the helm is recorded, but not a cracked skull.

Henry VIII jousted on countless occasions throughout his reign, from his coronation, at the birth of his son, Henry, who died after only a few months, during the Field of Cloth of Gold in Calais, to celebrate his marriage to Anne Boleyn and to celebrate the death of his first queen, Katherine, in 1536 – the final time Henry would joust.

MEN OF THE PRIVY CHAMBER

The young Henry was a true Renaissance prince. He had a love of art and architecture, could play and compose music (with varying degrees of success) spoke several languages and loved to discuss theology. But he was also fantastically fit and blessed with an athletic build, and he ensured that the men who served him from his Privy Chamber were equally handsome young men with whom he could hunt, joust, gamble, drink, and woo the occasional young woman.

Henry would rather spend a day hunting with his close friends than in a Privy Council meeting, and as a result they wielded enormous influence over the young king. The men, derided as 'minions', often ignored protocol and overstepped their boundaries with the king, much to Wolsey's chagrin. As Henry aged, he continued to appoint young men who made him feel as though he, too, was still a young man. But being close to the centre of power was a double-edged sword. Some of Henry's Gentlemen of the Privy Chamber enjoyed hugely successful careers, others faced the axeman, and even worse.

WILLIAM COMPTON

Despite being what historian Polydore Vergil described as the '*primus minister in regis cubiculo*' – premier member of the Privy Chamber and Groom of the Stool – William Compton does not appear in Mantel's series. Compton was a ward of Henry VII and grew up alongside the young Prince Henry. Understandably, they forged an enduring relationship, as he became Henry's most trusted companion. Compton was not unlike the young king – blond, tall and slender. Considered to be handsome and athletic, Compton was as physically active as his young king, and dedicated to leisurely pursuits. Yet the amount of power Compton wielded once Henry VIII ascended the throne was unprecedented. Henry gifted him several highly lucrative positions, including Lord Chancellor of Ireland, Sheriff of Worcestershire and Sheriff of Somerset, and Compton would manage more royal estates than any other courtier.

Crucially, his appointment as Groom of the Stool made him the closest companion Henry had in his inner chambers. Compton made use of this position – he was something of a gatekeeper and would act as intermediary if the royal signature was required; even Wolsey had to go via Compton. But for courtiers he was a founder of fortunes, and any courtier who sought favour or position at court approached Compton first. It is impossible to know how Compton's career or friendship with Henry would have fared under the pressure of his courtship with Anne. In 1528, Compton was among thousands, including Anne Boleyn and her father Thomas, to catch the sweating sickness – they recovered, but Compton did not survive. While mourned, his death opened up a prime position in the Privy Chamber but also allowed other young men to enjoy Henry's favour and patronage.

HENRY NORRIS

Henry Norris, born in 1482, was nine years older than the king, and one of the oldest men in Henry's inner circle. He began his career as a page and worked his way up, landing a position as a Gentleman of the Privy Chamber in 1517, a place from where he would enjoy Henry's favour and thereby accrue land and offices. Henry Norris was a popular man at court, renowned for his jousting abilities and athleticism, which is likely why Henry chose him for the highly coveted position of Groom of the Stool in 1526. In the series, Norris is a hard man to read, and Cromwell distrusts his easy-going charm. We first come across him in *Wolf Hall*, riding hard to overtake the disgraced Cardinal in order to deliver a message from Henry. Norris gives Wolsey the king's ring, causing Wolsey to jump from off his mule and into the mud, crying, Cromwell notes. It is a sight Cromwell will not forget, his master in the mud, with a man he feels is false and disingenuous.

Historically, Norris had a reputation at court for being a man of integrity and chivalry – we see this when Henry VIII deliberately humiliated Wolsey after the disastrous Legatine trial by having no room reserved for him when he and Cardinal Campeggio visited the King, and it was Norris who quietly offered Wolsey his own room. Norris belonged to a personal echelon of court, which not even Cromwell could penetrate; it was a battle for influence.

We see this in *Bring Up the Bodies*, when the king is escorting Imperial ambassador Chapuys into his chambers, and Cromwell seeks to follow:

But here is Norris blocking his path. In his Moorish drapery, his face blacked, he is playful, smiling, but still vigilant.

To the historical and fictional Cromwell, Norris was a charming man who needed to be removed from Henry's sphere of influence.

ANTHONY DENNY

Anthony Denny, an ally of Cromwell's (and enemy of Stephen Gardiner's), does not appear in Mantel's series, but he was one of the more educated and well-to-do young men of the Privy Chamber. Denny was one of the king's closest confidants, and while he was not appointed to the Privy Chamber until quite late in his career – 1539 – he was granted lucrative positions, including Keeper of the Privy Purse, and would serve as Henry's last Groom of the Stool. Denny was an experienced diplomat as well as an accomplished soldier, and joined Henry on his military campaigns to France in the 1540s.

It was to Denny that Henry confessed he was not attracted to the wife Cromwell had procured for him – Anne of Cleves. It was also Denny who helped finalize Henry's will in 1547, and bravely told the king he should prepare for death.

Francis Bryan

A half-cousin of both Anne Boleyn and Jane Seymour, Francis Bryan, known as the 'Vicar of Hell' for his lack of scruples, was one of the chief men of Henry's Privy Chamber. Bryan enjoyed several influential posts, including Esquire of the Body, but he was notorious for his rowdy behaviour and for overstepping his friendship with the king, and Wolsey had him removed twice from the Privy Chamber in what was known as 'the expulsion of the minions', once in 1529 and again in 1526. That year, Bryan lost an eye in a jousting accident and wore an eye patch, which may have been why he was allowed back into the inner sanctum of the Privy Chamber. We see Bryan and Cromwell working together throughout *Bring Up the Bodies* to bring Anne down. But the alliance, as we see in *The Mirror and the Light*, is short-lived as Mantel's Cromwell is not overly fond of Bryan: 'Sir Francis is intermittently pious, as conspicuous sinners tend to be.'

Mantel describes Byran as an undiplomatic diplomat; certainly Bryan's reputation preceded him. Appointed as an ambassador to France, he was quickly recalled due to his gambling and drunken behaviour, and Henry never appointed him again. Instead, he became the go-to man for other peculiar and less savoury missions.

Thomas Culpepper

Mantel's Cromwell has little time for Thomas Culpepper, who crops up in *The Mirror and the Light*, but historically Culpepper, an ambitious young man who was also a cousin of both Anne Boleyn and Catherine Howard, had several ties to the Cromwells – his older brother was a client of Cromwell and Culpepper had worked with Richard Cromwell.

Culpepper rose through the courtier ranks, becoming a favourite of Henry VIII's, despite a shocking accusation that he had raped the wife of a park keeper and murdered her husband (though this may have been his older brother, also called Thomas). In any event, Culpepper was elevated to the coveted Privy Chamber. Mantel's Cromwell would not be alive to witness the scandal which engulfed Henry's fifth Queen, Catherine, who was executed for (alleged) adultery with Culpepper and another man, Francis Dereham, who she had known prior to her marriage to Henry. Culpepper met his end at Tyburn, suffering a traitor's death.

FRANCIS WESTON

Sir Francis Weston was one of the younger members of Henry's inner circle and came from a respectable family – his father, Sir Richard Weston, had served as Under-Treasurer of the Exchequer and his mother had served as one of Katherine of Aragon's ladies-in-waiting.

Like Norris and George Boleyn, Weston began his career at court serving as a page, but his love of hunting, gambling and other sports quickly endeared him to a king who was beginning to age, and he was appointed as a Gentleman of the Privy Chamber. In 1533 he was knighted at Anne Boleyn's coronation, and would likely have had a long career in Henry's service, had he not been caught up in the violent events of 1536.

WILLIAM BRERETON

William Brereton was of a well-to-do family – his father, Sir Randle Brereton, had served as a knight under Henry VII. By 1521 he had become a Groom of the Chamber, and several years later, was promoted to the Privy Chamber. But Brereton had an unsavoury reputation according to George Cavendish, who accused him of persecuting innocent people – there was a story of one John ap Griffith Eyton who was hanged in 1534 because Brereton believed he killed one of his retainers. Eyton had been acquitted but Brereton persuaded Anne Boleyn to intervene, and the man was arrested once more and executed, despite Cromwell's efforts on his behalf.

Indeed, it would seem that Cromwell had issues with almost every member of the Privy Chamber:

I have probably, he thinks, gone as far as I can to accommodate them.
Now they must accommodate me, or be removed.
(Bring Up the Bodies)

3
A NEW ERA

THE CARDINAL'S DESCENT

At Hampton Court in the great hall they perform an interlude; its name is
'The Cardinal's Descent into Hell'. (Wolf Hall)

In this scene the 'entertainment' features men dressed as devils stabbing
a scarlet-clad figure with tridents. This is a pivotal moment in *Wolf Hall*;
Wolsey is dead. Weeks prior, on 1 November 1530, the commission for
Wolsey's arrest was given to Henry Percy, now Earl of Northumberland.
Wolsey had not yet reached York when Percy visited him at Cawood in North
Yorkshire, greeting him with the warrant. He was to return to London and
to the Tower; Anne had got her way at last. But Wolsey's enemies would be
denied the pleasure of seeing the once-great Lord Chancellor executed – he
fell ill on the journey south and died near Leicester Abbey where he was
buried, metres from the grave of Richard III. We do not know how deeply
Cromwell mourned his master, but we can speculate. Certainly Mantel's
Cromwell finds it unbearable to hear of Wolsey's last days from an equally
distraught George Cavendish, with feelings of guilt surging through him that
he had been preoccupied with court matters, and was not there at such a time.

He cannot openly lament, but he goes to his drawer and opens a package
the Cardinal had given him before he left for the north. In it is the Cardinal's
turquoise ring, which Cromwell had always admired, the very ring we see
in Cromwell's famous portrait. Eyes at court also recognize the ring, and
though he doesn't say it the meaning is clear: he will always be Wolsey's man.
Wolsey's death weighing on him, Cromwell watches with the court as they
shriek in amusement at the play.

Historically, however, the details of the farce are lost, and it is unclear just
what it entailed, whether it was it a dance, a monologue or a play. Originally it
was ambassador Chapuys who reported that Thomas Boleyn 'caused a farce
to be acted of the Cardinal going down to Hell'. But far from a public display,
this was a private scene of entertainment for Boleyn's guest – the French
ambassador, Gabriel de Grammont, during a private dinner. It was, however,
the Duke of Norfolk who then had the farce printed and publicized. In
Wolf Hall, Cromwell quietly moves behind the curtains and takes note of
the actors – George Boleyn, Henry Norris, Francis Weston and William
Brereton. He will remember their positions in that play for years to come.

Despite his heartbreak at Wolsey's demise and death, Cromwell smoothly
made the transition from Wolsey's service to that of the king, and by the
beginning of 1531, when Cromwell was sworn in as a royal councillor, he must

have felt he had reached the pinnacle of his career. In *Wolf Hall*, Thomas More warns, 'Now you are a member of the council, I hope you will tell the king what he ought to do, not merely what he can do. If the lion knew his own strength, it would be hard to rule him.'

The years between 1530 and 1533 were fraught with difficulty as Henry battled two women – his queen, Katherine, who he was determined to be rid of, and his mistress, Anne, who he struggled to please. Now, finding himself a part of the Privy Council, Cromwell would spend his time trying to extricate Henry from his first marriage. Mantel breezes through the details of certain events, for the marital landscape barely changed from 1527–31, but for Cromwell his career was going from strength to strength.

THOMAS MORE

Mantel's More is cruel, 'fussily pious', enjoys flogging beggars in his garden and sending people to the stake. Perhaps this is how Cromwell saw the man who would change neither his religion, nor his loyalty to the woman he considered to be queen, Katherine. But certainly Mantel's More has polarized opinion – for many he is almost unrecognizable from the traditional interpretation, especially in Robert Bolt's play, *A Man for All Seasons*. Perhaps that is the issue – Mantel's More is quite unlike the Thomas More of Robert Bolt's play, but that More is also a fictional construct, perched at the other end of the spectrum. Somewhere in between the fanatic and saint lies the real Thomas More. Of course, in *Wolf Hall* what Mantel has done is to capture some critical elements of the real More – from his use of profanity in his pamphlets against Luther:

You would not think that such words would proceed from Thomas More, but they do. No one has rendered the Latin tongue more obscene.

To his uncompromising approach to scripture:

He would chain you up, for a mistranslation. He would, for a difference in your Greek, kill you.

More was born in 1477, the same year as Thomas Boleyn. The son of John More, an attorney who later became a judge, More benefitted from his father's influence, and at the age of 12, More served as a page in the household of John Morton, Archbishop of Canterbury, who sent More to Oxford at the age of 14.

It is in Morton's household that Mantel imagines Cromwell and More meeting. Cromwell helped his uncle, who served in the kitchens of Bishop Morton's palace at Lambeth. Cromwell, only a young boy, had heard of the child prodigy about to leave for Oxford, and serves the 14-year-old More wheat bread. More has a book open, which arouses Cromwell's curiosity, and he asks what is in the book, to which the young More replies with a slightly patronizing smile, 'Words, words, just words.' For his part, More has no memory of the event, but Cromwell will not forget it.

Like Cromwell, More trained as a lawyer, working at the New Inn, as opposed to Gray's Inn where Cromwell was a member. More was torn between professions – he had a passion for literature and religious scripture and also entertained the notion of becoming a monk. Mantel's Cromwell speculates that he decided not to, however, for:

More would have been a priest, but human flesh called to him with its inconvenient demands.

It may be that More simply opted for a career in civil service. More entered Parliament in 1504, and began to work his way up. In 1514, he was elevated to Henry's Privy Council, and then to secretary and advisor to the king. Wolsey also helped facilitate his career, recommending that More be elected as Speaker in the House of Commons. During this time he wrote his famed *Utopia*, establishing himself as a scholar, but he was also an exceptional negotiator, and was part of a delegation dispatched to Bruges and Antwerp by Henry VIII to the court of Charles V, to secure protection for English merchants, and by 1521, More held the important post of Under-Treasurer of the Exchequer. Historically, More was well respected at court, was deeply liked and admired by many who considered him a friend and had a tremendous influence on Henry's own spiritual ideology (until More's ideology favoured Katherine) – we see More's influence in Henry's strongly worded rebuke of Martin Luther's teachings.

More married Jane Colt in 1505, and together they had four children. Unfortunately Jane died in 1511, and with peculiar speed, More married Alice Middleton a month later. More had no children from this second marriage, but he raised Alice's daughter from her previous marriage (also named Alice) as his own. More gave the girls the same classical education as his son, which was unusual for the time, and is a decision that can only be admired.

He was immensely proud of his children, and Margaret in particular, whose command of Greek and Latin delighted her father, who boasted of her linguistic skills. Mantel draws on the family theme, but it is somewhat twisted to suit her portrait of More. This More invites his guests to mock his wife and daughter-in-law, Anne, to the embarrassment of his guests, insulting his wife's looks and character, and also patronizing his children. But from the surviving correspondence between More and his children it is clear that they were a close-knit family.

Historically, More enjoyed the same close relationship with Henry that Wolsey did, though there is not the same degree of friction between More and Cromwell as is shown in *Wolf Hall*, nor is it clear how the real Cromwell felt about him – Mantel has fleshed out their relationship. Mantel's Cromwell dines with More on occasion, once both as guests at the house of their mutual friend, the Italian merchant, Antonio Bonvisi. The scene is tense, not just because fish is the only item on the Lenten menu, but because More was one of the prime movers against the Cardinal. Historically, More was highly critical of the Cardinal, addressing Parliament shortly after Wolsey's fall. In his address, More described Henry as a good shepherd and the Cardinal as a castrated male sheep, fraudulent and crafty. Apart from sending evangelicals to the stake, More has been accused of zealously torturing and flogging countless individuals he deemed as heretics. He denied such claims, and they cannot be substantiated, though Mantel's Cromwell believes it.

Later, Cromwell visits More at his house in Chelsea. As he enters he notes the now famous portrait of More and his family:

You see them painted life-size before you meet them in the flesh; and More, conscious of the double effect it makes, pauses, to let you survey them, to take them in.

Like Wolsey, More takes an interest in carpets, and invites his guests to admire his new purchase. More is pleased, but Cromwell's hands roam the knots and wefts, knowing its price immediately. Wolsey would not have paid a shilling for it.

More remained deeply loyal to Queen Katherine, and believed Henry's marriage was valid. In the first years of Henry's pursuit of a divorce, More remains silent, which he hopes will be enough for Henry. It is a stance that will backfire, as Henry begins to explore the depths of his power, aided by Anne Boleyn. The real Thomas More said it best when he compared having Henry's favour to playing with tamed lions – 'often it is harmless, often he roars in rage for no known reason, and suddenly the fun becomes fatal.'

THE AMBASSADOR

If we were to see Cromwell as he would want to be seen – that is, through his own papers – we would not get an inkling of the man. The intelligence, certainly, the ruthlessness, to be sure, and we owe a debt to his contemporaries, Cavendish and Hall. But there is another source – the Imperial ambassador, Eustace Chapuys. The relationship between Charles V's ambassador and Thomas Cromwell was most unexpected and complex, and it lasted right up until Cromwell's death.

Eustace Chapuys was born sometime around 1489 in the bustling market town of Annecy, which at the time belonged to the state of Savoy, and is now part of France. The eldest of six children, his parents, Louis and Guigone, had great ambitions for Eustace and ensured that he was well-educated, firstly in Annecy and later at the prestigious Turin University, where he completed his doctorate. Turin University had a sound reputation for legal training and was a lively centre of the emerging philosophy of humanism. History has tended to label Chapuys as devoutly – even zealously – Catholic, so it might come as a surprise to learn that he was actually part of an intellectual, humanist network that included well-known reformers, such as fellow Turin University student François Bonivard, the Swiss ecclesiastic religious reformer. He was also close to theologian Heinrich Cornelius Agrippa, as well as the scholar and humanist Erasmus, with whom he communicated for over a decade.

At some point, Chapuys went to Geneva, which was then an important political and religious centre and part of the Duchy of Savoy, where he was ordained. Geneva was a crucial stage for Chapuys, for it was here that the still relatively young lawyer would prove his strong work ethic and grasp of political and religious affairs. Most importantly, he would serve his apprenticeship in the art of diplomacy.

While in Geneva, Charles V, the Holy Roman Emperor, invited Chapuys to his court in Barcelona where he soon proved himself to be an invaluable diplomat (and why he became known as 'the Spanish Ambassador'). But what made him particularly valuable to Charles was his legal training because Charles V's aunt was Katherine of Aragon, Queen of England, and in 1529, she was under siege. Charles needed someone like Chapuys in England where unprecedented events were unfolding at Henry VIII's court.

Chapuys arrived in England in 1529, ready to do battle as the new resident ambassador and Katherine of Aragon's divorce lawyer, and for the next 16 years he witnessed some of the most dramatic events of Henry VIII's reign.

Chapuys became fiercely loyal, and his respect and admiration for Katherine far surpassed the requirements of his ambassadorial duties. As for Katherine, her admiration of her ambassador was evident in her correspondence with her nephew Charles.

'You could not have chosen a better ambassador; his wisdom encourages and comforts me, and when my councillors through fear hesitate to answer the charges against me, he is always ready to undertake the burden of my defence ... I consider him deserving of all your favour.'

We first glimpse Mantel's Chapuys at the same dinner attended by Cromwell and Thomas More, at the home of Italian merchant Antonio Bonvisi, where Chapuys is a late arrival:

He stands poised on the threshold ... a little crooked man, in a doublet slashed and puffed, blue satin billowing through black; beneath it, his little black spindly legs.

We cannot remark with any certainty the state of Chapuys' lower extremities, but his portraits suggest he was slender, with dark, beady eyes and short cropped hair. But from his dispatches, which number in the thousands, we see the elegant turns of phrase of a talented ambassador.

In Mantel's books we do not get a sense of just how much Cromwell fascinated the ambassador – Chapuys spent many reports simply detailing all he knew about Cromwell, and from these an interesting portrait of Cromwell emerges: an astute man who had a rather disarming nature, shrewd, frank, ambitious and highly intelligent.

At the dinner described in *Wolf Hall*, Chapuys has no interest in Cromwell, choosing to speak to Thomas More instead. Historically Chapuys did spend more time with conservatives at court including the Duke of Norfolk, but he must have started to notice Cromwell as the latter's responsibilities grew, and soon he began to see Cromwell as a friend and ally, someone whom he was determined to keep on side. In his first years at court, there was tentative communication between the two, with Chapuys attempting to gain Cromwell's trust slowly. Cromwell, it seemed, had exactly the same idea. Nevertheless, Chapuys told Charles V hopefully that he was determined to 'set the net, and see if I cannot catch him; I will nevertheless keep a good look-out ahead and risk nothing without being well prepared, knowing, as I do, that in these matters one cannot be too cautious.'

Mantel's Cromwell looks on Chapuys with humour, and there is something comical about the way he is portrayed, seemingly naive and unaware when he is being played. In reality, Chapuys usually knew exactly what was happening, but openly chose to engage. Perhaps then Mantel's description is not far off the mark:

He is like a man who has wandered inadvertently into a play, who has found it to be a comedy, and decided to stay and see it through.

Nevertheless, the two men – the radical lateral thinker and conservative ambassador – had much in common. They were both lawyers who had lived in Italy, and they shared similar tastes and ideals, and quite fortuitously, they were neighbours, living at St Katherine's, now known as St Katherine's Docks, near the Tower of London; the two households often came together when Chapuys and Cromwell dined – something Chapuys does very well in *The Mirror and The Light*. Surprisingly, they hunted together, lent each other books, and walked together in various palace gardens discussing tapestries, art, scholarship, Italy and wider European politics. Mantel suggests that Chapuys never learned English, and could only rely on those conversations in French, which he could understand, but here she does not give him enough credit.

After four years in England Chapuys claimed he still could not entirely follow a rapid conversation in English. However, he was a shrewd diplomat and rather suspiciously made much fuss about having trouble with understanding English at court. In fact, Chapuys was linguistically gifted – he spoke German, Spanish, Italian, Flemish, Latin and a little Greek – and French was his native tongue. Chapuys is often described as rather gossipy, but his invaluable letters and reports give life to this period. Mantel clearly thought so too, for she plucks scenes for her books from Chapuys' own dispatches.

In an audience with a volatile Henry VIII, one of many in which Henry's treatment of Katherine of Aragon and obsession with Anne Boleyn is discussed, the king asks Chapuys what he thinks his motives are for divorcing Katherine and the break with Rome. Chapuys responds:

Kill a cardinal? Divide your country? Split the church? 'Seems extravagant,' Chapuys murmurs.

Henry's reaction is dramatic: he berates Chapuys, bursting into angry tears. Mantel observes:

He is a game little terrier, the Emperor's man; but even he knows that when you've made a king cry it's time to back off.

In 1533, a fire devastated the ambassador's rather fine lodgings by the Tower. The blaze was so fierce that neither Chapuys nor his household had any time to save valuables. Chapuys lost everything: his gold plate, clothes, furniture from Italy, which he had prized, and sentimental personal effects. But new lodgings were quickly found, and Cromwell likely played a part in finding the new house, which was a stone's throw from one of his own luxurious and favourite houses.

Their masters may have had a strained relationship – Katherine of Aragon and Anne Boleyn were the main points of contention – but the ambassador and Cromwell remained firm friends. Mantel illustrates this beautifully:

Officially, he and the ambassador are barely on speaking terms. Unofficially, Chapuys sends him a vat of good olive oil. He retaliates with capons. The ambassador himself arrives, followed by a retainer carrying a parmesan cheese.

When they are in private, they dispense with their 'masks of dissimulation' as Chapuys called it. Through Chapuys' dispatches, sometimes paraphrased by Mantel, we are offered a glimpse of Cromwell's sly charm. When discussing the Emperor's possible response to Henry's preparation for war towards the end of *Wolf Hall*, Cromwell says:

'... Oh, I know his coffers are bottomless. The Emperor could ruin us all if he liked.' He smiles. 'But what good would that do the Emperor?'

As the years progressed, the real Chapuys evolved at court as his mission shifted from defending Katherine to protecting her daughter Mary, which brought him even more in line with Cromwell.

THE PRIVY COUNCIL AT WESTMINSTER

Geoffrey Elton described the Privy Council as 'the instrument of policy making, the arena of political conflict, and the ultimate means for dispensing the king's justice.' Under Cromwell, the once-large Privy Council was significantly reformed and restructured, with many nobles losing their position. Cromwell dominated the council, but attempted to build a power base of allies and those he considered friends to balance the remaining detractors – it was a rare but grave miscalculation.

THOMAS AUDLEY

Described in *Wolf Hall* as a man whose 'convictions are flexible', Thomas Audley (sometimes spelled Audeley) was one of the most adaptable men of the period. Someone who seemed to take nothing personally, and expected others to feel the same, he changed allegiances without a qualm.

Born in Essex in 1488, he was the son-in-law of Cromwell's first employer, Thomas Grey. It is believed that Audley first attended Cambridge to study law, before entering Middle Temple, London. He also pursued a career in Parliament, joining as an MP for Essex and becoming a Justice of the Peace while climbing the ladder at court, being appointed Groom of the Chamber in 1527, answering to the Lord Chamberlain. Audley had been a personal and political supporter of Cardinal Wolsey since entering his service in 1527, where he met Cromwell, who called Audley 'oon of my grettest frendes'. Audley was elected Speaker of the House of Commons, and presided over the Reformation Parliament, which sat from 1529 until 1536. He was a firm advocate of abolishing papal jurisdiction and was instrumental in the dissolution of the monasteries, from which he benefited enormously. Audley supported Henry's annulment and was part of the Boleyns' sphere. When Thomas More resigned his position, it was Cromwell who recommended Audley be appointed as Keeper of the Great Seal.

In 1533, Audley reached the pinnacle of his career, being appointed Lord Chancellor, and he and Cromwell worked together for years as a political dream team. But, when Cromwell lost favour, it was Audley who was instrumental in creating the act of attainder against his former friend. Audley proved that his loyalty to the king trumped all else.

STEPHEN GARDINER

Stephen Gardiner was a complex figure, historically as inscrutable as he is in the series. A man of contradictions – he was no fan of Anne Boleyn, protested

Henry's break with Rome, and yet he defended Henry's title as Supreme Head of the Church, which may have added to his reputation. Several contemporaries described Gardiner and their depictions seem to correspond. He was by many accounts (including his own) crafty, wily and cunning. The son of a clothmaker in Bury St Edmunds, Suffolk, Gardiner transcended his humble beginnings to attend Cambridge, where he excelled in classical studies and became devoted to the study of canon and civil law. Rumours always swirled around Gardiner's lineage. It was said that Gardiner was the illegitimate grandson of Jasper Tudor, Henry VIII's great-uncle, making him a cousin of the king, if the stories were indeed true.

But his entrée into the Tudor court came with a position in the household of the Duke of Norfolk, serving as a tutor to his son, before being appointed as a secretary to Cardinal Wolsey sometime in 1524. Both Gardiner and Cromwell were diligent and hard-working, and the Cardinal relied on them considerably, but they were bitter rivals, an enmity which began in the Cardinal's household, though the reasons are never completely clear. Mantel supposes envy to be the cause:

Master Stephen resents everything about his own situation ... that he's the king's unacknowledged cousin ... that he was put into the church ... that someone else has late-night talks with the cardinal, to whom he is confidential secretary.

The two men would remain diametrically opposed politically, with Gardiner protesting Henry's break with Rome and rejecting Cromwell's radical attempts to reform the Church. Unlike Cromwell, Gardiner's expertise lay in canon law, which would make him indispensable to Henry VIII and his 'great matter'. Gardiner was an accomplished diplomat, and in 1527 he was appointed to a commission alongside Thomas More to arrange a treaty with the French and to assist French troops fighting Charles V in Italy. He also accompanied Cardinal Wolsey on his important diplomatic mission to France, to gain French favour for Henry's divorce from Katherine. Wolsey's reliance on Gardiner was evident when he rejected orders from Henry for Gardiner to return to England for fresh instructions. Wolsey insisted that he could not spare Gardiner, who was the only instrument he had in advancing Henry's cause.

Wolsey also sent Gardiner on a mission to Orvieto, Italy, where Pope Clement had taken refuge following the sack of Rome, with the unenviable task of trying to secure permission to allow a papal legate to preside over an English trial alongside Wolsey.

Despite the Cardinal's favour and patronage, it is suggested in Mantel's series that Gardiner showed little loyalty to the Cardinal, though evidence shows that he served Wolsey to the best of his ability. When Wolsey fell in 1529, Gardiner replaced his former master as the king's Secretary, and in 1531 Gardiner was appointed to Cardinal Wolsey's former bishopric, Winchester, one of the country's wealthiest dioceses. However, Gardiner's contradictory attitude towards the divorce and Henry's break with Rome meant that he would struggle to retain Henry's favour and was never trusted completely.

Gardiner showed every sign of rising, but he often shot himself in the foot, making terrible miscalculations. The first occurred in March 1532, when he led the charge against the Supplication of the Commons against the Ordinaries, which was a list of grievances against the English church by parliament that had been drafted by Cromwell. Gardiner objected to the clauses, writing a personal defence to the king, infuriating Henry:

Henry rages about Gardiner: disloyalty, he shouts, ingratitude. Can he remain my Secretary, when he has set himself up in direct opposition to me?

Gardiner, perhaps, did not anticipate Henry's anger, but he likely got the message when the Archbishop of Canterbury, William Warham, died in 1533, and the hopeful Gardiner was overlooked in favour of the man he had introduced to court, Thomas Cranmer. He struggles to regain his influence at court, losing his position as Secretary to the King in 1534, to none other than Thomas Cromwell. Mantel's Cromwell hopes to see the last of Gardiner, but as the latter complained of Cromwell – that he had a habit of resurfacing – Cromwell would find the same of his enemy.

With Cromwell's demise in 1540, Gardiner set his sights on Cranmer, who, unlike his fallen friend, had powerful allies in the Seymour brothers. Gardiner was ultimately unable to reconcile his own Catholic beliefs with the reforms sweeping the country under Edward VI, for which he was imprisoned and deprived of his bishopric. He must have felt a deep sense of relief when he was released during Mary's reign and pleased to see England restored to Catholicism – and Cranmer destroyed.

THOMAS 'CALL ME RISLEY' WRIOTHESLEY

The London-born Thomas Wriothesley was the grandson of John Writh, a Garter King of Arms, and son of William Wryth, a York herald. At some point his father and uncle chose to change the name from 'Wryth' to 'Wriothesley', believed to be a more noble line.

Wriothesley studied civil law at Cambridge and was a protégé of Stephen Gardiner, whom he followed into Wolsey's household, where he also met Thomas Cromwell. In 1529 he was appointed as clerk of the Cofferer of the Household, moving up to an appointment as one of the Clerks of the Signet for Gardiner. He then worked for Cromwell when he replaced Gardiner as Secretary, and whatever his loyalties may have been to the latter, he became a firm member of Cromwell's camp. In the series, Cromwell goes to great lengths to win Wriothesley, at first only intending to use him to spy on Gardiner, but they develop a close connection, with Cromwell trusting Wriothesley with sensitive tasks over the years. Mantel places Wriothesley in Cromwell's home on numerous occasions, detailing scenes of families coming together, in particular Christmas of 1535, when Wriothesley attends Christmas at Cromwell's house with his wife and young daughter. Wriothesley would remain one of his right-hand men, or so Cromwell believed. Wriothesley's ability to switch horses saw his career flourish even more post-Cromwell, becoming one of Henry's leading councillors.

TURNING POINT

On 5 January 1531, an extraordinary papal brief reached court, stating that, at Katherine's request, the pope forbade Henry to remarry 'until the decision of the case, and declares that if he does all issue will be illegitimate. It forbids any one in England, of ecclesiastical or secular dignity, universities, parliaments, courts of law, &c., from making any decision in the affair, the judgement of which is reserved for the Holy See. The whole under pain of excommunication.'

Thomas Cranmer

Henry, with Cromwell by his side, had already begun to consider other options. Wolsey's failure to secure an annulment in the legatine trial opened the door to others to try more innovative approaches, and it was Stephen Gardiner who first drew Henry's attention to a young theologian, Thomas Cranmer, who, like everyone else throughout the country, had followed the legatine trial at Blackfriars. The story goes that Gardiner, Cranmer and Edward Fox, Gardiner's ambassadorial colleague, spoke of the 'great matter' over supper one evening, and Cranmer advised that the problem with the annulment was its approach. Cranmer suggested that it was not an issue of canon law, but a theological issue. He believed that the theologians of universities both in England and abroad should be consulted on the legitimacy of Henry's marriage, which Fox relayed to the king. Cranmer was sent to Durham House, Thomas Boleyn's residence in the Strand, where he could have time to write, and access to books, suggesting Thomas Boleyn's library was well stocked. We know of Cranmer's loyalty to Anne, but he was also deeply devoted to Thomas Boleyn, remaining a trusted and loyal confidant until the latter's death in 1539.

As Diarmaid MacCulloch writes, Cromwell and Cranmer were linked by two ultimately incompatible ideals, loyalty to the king and their passion for an evangelical reformation, yet MacCulloch believes that theirs was an uncommonly close and sincere friendship, though this has been disputed by other historians. Cranmer attended Cambridge in 1503 and was elected to a fellowship at Jesus College, which he had to relinquish when he married a young pregnant widow named Joan. Joan would not survive the birth, and while Jesus College restored Cranmer to his fellowship, it likely felt like a hollow reward. Cranmer entered the church and quickly developed a reputation as an astute theologian, but he also began to entertain notions which many would view as heretical. He often met with a group of scholars who discussed Martin Luther's teachings and were vocal in their dissatisfaction with the abuse of the clergy. Some of the men with whom Cranmer mixed were also known to Cromwell and play a part in Mantel's series, including William Tyndale, the English scholar who would, in a sense, become the face of the English Reformation, famed for his translation of the New Testament into English, and Thomas Bilney, nicknamed 'Little Bilney' due to his short stature.

SUPREMACY

By 1531, Henry had secured the scholarly opinions of the various universities of Europe, which Thomas More presented to the House of Commons in March. It was made into a book called *Censurae academiarum* which Cranmer translated into English, providing a snapshot of scholarly opinion, though it was by no means a comprehensive survey.

The events of 1531 are only alluded to in Mantel's series but they are significant. Parliament's main goal was to secure a mandate to consider the 'manifold abuses of the clergy' – Henry charged the members of the English Church with praemunire with a hefty fine of £100,000 to buy a pardon.

When Mantel's Cromwell visits Queen Katherine and her daughter Mary, she is well informed on the matter. She reflects on the charge made against Cardinal Wolsey and compares it to the latest attack on the English clergy and the fine that was imposed alongside it. Cromwell responds, 'Not a fine. We call it a benevolence.' Henry demanded more, insisting that the clergy recognize that they held no jurisdiction independently of the crown.

Katherine and Mary are also aware that the clergy have bestowed on Henry the title of 'singular protector, supreme lord, and supreme head of the English church and clergy'. But while the bishops acknowledged Henry as Supreme Head of the Church and Clergy in England, a limiting clause, 'as far as the law of Christ allows', was added to Henry's new title.

In *Wolf Hall*, Cromwell is visiting the pair to inform them that Katherine and Mary are to be sent to the More, a palace in Hertfordshire, once owned by Wolsey. What Cromwell does not know is that Henry has already decided to separate mother and daughter.

Master Cromwell

By 1532, Cromwell was everywhere at court, but had no official post. Mantel imagines a frank conversation between Cromwell and Mary Boleyn, who is to convey Cromwell's private ambitions to the Lady Anne. He wants an official role in the royal household:

She nods. 'She made Tom Wyatt a poet. She made Harry Percy a madman. I'm sure she has some ideas about what to make you.'

In April of 1532, Cromwell was appointed Master of the Jewels and in July appointed as Clerk of the Hanaper, part of the office of the Chancery, though whether this was Anne's doing is debatable. Cromwell had become a central figure at court and a constant presence at Henry's side.

In March 1532, Cromwell's Supplication of the Commons against the Ordinaries, which Gardiner so opposed, was delivered to Parliament and the clergy, alleging that the English clergy's oaths to the Pope were a violation of their oaths to the crown. Parliament and the clergy reluctantly agreed rather than face charges of treason, but the fallout was immediate. Thomas More resigned as Lord Chancellor, unable to endorse the direction in which Henry was leading the church. He was not alone.

ELIZABETH BARTON: THE HOLY MAID OF KENT

Elizabeth Barton was something of a mystery. She was born sometime in 1506, and served in the household of Thomas Cobb, a farmer and land agent of the Archbishop of Canterbury, William Warham. She was destined to live an unremarkable life, but in 1525 she began to suffer from fits, falling into trances and having visions. She would speak for hours about the church, heaven and hell, and began to make prophecies, which was a sure way to gain attention. Soon enough, her fame reached the ears of Archbishop Warham, who, upon hearing of some of her miraculous visions, placed Barton as a nun in the Benedictine priory of St Sepulchre in Canterbury, under his protection. In 1528, Barton announced she wanted to meet Cardinal Wolsey, at that time still the most powerful prelate in England – her motives may be guessed at. Wolsey agreed to meet her, and while her message was hardly what he wanted to hear – that God had revealed to her that Henry's divorce from Katherine was contrary to His will, he was impressed enough to arrange a meeting between Barton and the king. By now Barton was on a roll – upon meeting with Henry in person, she boldly declared that an angel had appeared to her and told her that if he married Anne, he would risk the wrath of God. Henry good-naturedly ignored her words, but the next year she had another vision, which she shared with thousands of followers, before deciding Henry needed to hear it in person, which he would whether he wished to or not. It seemed like Anne and Henry could not venture anywhere near Canterbury without coming across Barton or her followers.

In 1532, Henry, Anne and the court travelled to the coast on their way to Calais, and they stopped briefly in Canterbury. While walking in a monastery garden, Barton intercepted them, failing to show any deference. Mantel places Cromwell in Henry's entourage as Barton accosts the couple to deliver her crushing prediction. 'And if you enter into a form of marriage with this unworthy woman, you will not reign seven months.'

By the end of 1533, despite Anne and Henry being married and with a healthy child in the cradle, Barton and her supporters continued to attack the king, so Cromwell made his move.

In *Wolf Hall* Barton is brought to Cromwell who, together with Cranmer, Richard Rich and Thomas Audley, question her intensely. Before long, Barton has a rather convenient vision that 'God willed her, by his heavenly messenger, that she should say that she never had revelation of God.'

And Cranmer reports that she confessed she had imagined everything to 'obtain worldly praise', though much of Barton's confession comes to us from Cromwell's notes. Cromwell and his colleagues needed to destroy her reputation, and on 23rd November Barton made a full confession before a crowd of several thousand, begging the king for mercy. She would repeat this performance through numerous towns around the country. Mantel's Cromwell visits Barton while she is imprisoned, half hoping she will implicate more people – even Queen Katherine – in her confessions.

Once they were satisfied she had outlived her usefulness, Henry made an example of her. On 20 April 1534, Barton was taken from her cell in the Tower of London where she had been imprisoned for several months, and dragged behind a horse for 5 miles (8km), from the Tower to Tyburn, where she was hanged and then strangled to death in front of a large crowd who came to witness the spectacle. She was then decapitated, her head boiled and set on a spike on London Bridge. Whether her visions were genuine or contrived, Cromwell knew she was too much of a rallying point to be allowed to live.

CALAIS

While Barton was still alive and showing off her divine talents around the country, Henry and his councillors had begun to look for foreign support for Henry's annulment and marriage to Anne. Options were limited as there was really only Charles V, who as Katherine's nephew was not a contender as an ally, or Francis I. It had been almost 12 years since the two kings had come face to face in France at the Field of Cloth of Gold, but by 1531 they were both older and were not willing to spend entire fortunes on an event that could come to nothing, which is exactly what had happened all those years previously. But a meeting between Anne and Henry, and Francis and his queen, Eleanor, would be an important stepping stone showing all of Europe that Henry's actions were legitimate, and that Anne should be his rightful queen. Immediately Henry faced an awkward issue: Eleanor was the sister of Charles V, and familial loyalty made a meeting between the two women almost impossible. Francis, who was trying to be helpful but missed the point entirely, suggested that he too bring his mistress, Madame de Vendôme, a suggestion that was immediately refused.

It was finally decided that Anne and her ladies would remain in Calais, while Henry and his male courtiers would ride on to meet Francis at

Boulogne. Before they could leave, it was decided that Anne required a change in title in order to be presented in France as Henry's future queen. In September 1532, Cromwell and the court witnessed her elevation in a grand ceremony at Windsor to the Marchioness of Pembroke, making her a peer in her own right.

For this important occasion Anne was determined to be attired as befitting a queen of England, and decided she would feel far closer to the throne if she were wearing the queen's jewels, many of which were still in Katherine's possession, and some that were actually gifts from Katherine's mother. But these were technicalities, and Norfolk was sent to fetch them. At first Katherine declared that she would not give up her jewels to 'ornament a person who is the scandal of Christendom'. But if it was an express command, she would relinquish them. Perhaps she imagined Henry would not go so far, but the command came swiftly. By late 1532 Cromwell was flourishing. Mantel's Cromwell marvels at how far he has come:

Anne refers everything to him; she says, laughing, 'Cromwell, you are my man.' The wind is set fair and the tide is running for him. He can feel the tug of it under his feet.

The English landed in Calais on Friday 11 October, and five days later, Norfolk, Thomas Boleyn and group of gentlemen met with 'the great mayster of Fraunce', Anne, duc de Montmorency, in Boulogne before returning to Calais.

Historically Anne was frustrated at being left behind: Francis had no women in his train and therefore Anne and her ladies could not be present. But it was Anne, with her perfect command of French, her charm and vivaciousness, and her knowledge of the French court and its king, who would be an asset at any French meeting.

Francis and Henry return to Calais where they attend a lavish supper for both courts. After the feast, Anne and her ladies surprise the court, emerging in gowns of 'straunge fashion, made of clothe of gold'. Mantel's Anne is seductive, enticing Francis to sit in a window bay to talk. There is something almost inappropriate about her version, seen through Cromwell's eyes, and he enlists Norfolk to tear Anne and the French king away from one another:

'My lord, fetch your niece away. She has done enough diplomacy. Our king is jealous.'

This, of course, is partially artistic license. By all accounts, Anne spoke with great affection for France, of her time there, and implored Francis to support their cause, but Mantel is setting the scene for us. Cromwell watches as an infuriated Anne is dragged away by her uncle, with Henry watching in angry satisfaction that she will be punished by her family for wanton behaviour.

Cromwell then hears doors slamming, voices raised. Mary Shelton, a cousin of the Boleyns and Anne's lady-in-waiting, rushes out of her rooms in search of a Bible – Anne is demanding one. Cromwell meets Mary Boleyn in the gardens, who tells him that at last Anne and Henry have consummated their relationship. Cromwell asks what the Bible was needed for:

'To swear him. Before witnesses. Me. Norris. He made a binding promise. They are married in God's sight. And he swears he will marry her again in England and crown her queen when spring comes.'

Exactly when Henry and Anne first slept together has filled countless pages of history books – no other consummation, save Katherine of Aragon's, has been so scrutinized – but it was not the result of a jealous quarrel between the couple. After a thoroughly successful series of meetings and banquets, the English had planned to sail from Calais to Dover, but the winds had whipped up the waters of the English Channel and the ships turned back. They were stranded for eight days, as the harbour was besieged by storms and mist. It is believed that during this time, the couple consummated their relationship, and upon their return to England, they were secretly wed, either in late 1532 or early 1533.

A WAY FORWARD

In the hall of Austin Friars, Mantel's Cromwell is having his coat of arms painted on the wall. The German painter is painting a rose, lions, and two blackbirds – the blackbirds are Wolsey's emblem. By 1533, in Mantel's words, Cromwell is minister of everything. He certainly was a prominent member of the council and at court, and seemed the ideal royal servant. 'Sometimes it is a solace to me,' Henry says, 'not to have to talk and talk. You were born to understand me, perhaps.'

In the series, Cromwell conducts all business and oversees anything of importance; he stands quietly as a witness to Anne and Henry's secret marriage in England, confirming the promises they made in Calais. He spies Mary Boleyn, who holds up a hand, her fingers an inch apart. It is the only sign so far that Anne is pregnant.

In *Wolf Hall*, Cromwell has become indispensable to Anne, but he remains wary and distant. She will forever in his eyes be a creature of calculation, and Mantel's Cromwell often makes references to an unsavoury reputation with men, a reputation the real Anne did not have prior to the accusations of 1536. Historically, Anne and Cromwell's relationship is a complex and ever-shifting one; they are politically and religiously aligned, but there is no evidence that the two were particularly close. But one wonders if the ever-cautious Cromwell was hesitant to get too close to the Boleyn circle – they were now all in uncharted territory, Henry was technically a bigamist, and the child Anne carried risked being seen as illegitimate. As Rafe Sadler quietly reminds Cromwell: '... the whole history of the king's marriage tells us a child in the womb is not an heir in the cradle.'

TRIUMPH

Henry's hand was forced by Anne's condition, which was a blessing in disguise. When the Archbishop of Canterbury, William Warham, died in 1532, it left a vacancy in the powerful diocese, and Henry and Anne knew exactly who should fill it. Henry breezily nominated 'a nobody', in Rome's eyes – Thomas Cranmer – and Clement, eager to please Henry, quickly gave his consent for Cranmer to be consecrated as archbishop, and the papal bulls were drawn up. Chapuys hastily wrote to Clement, advising him to delay the bulls until after the case had reached a verdict in Rome, so that Cranmer's involvement could be neutralized and the matter not brought to England. Chapuys, who rarely missed a trick, also informed Clement just who Cranmer was, but he was ignored. Matters moved with impressive speed. In late March the bulls for the archbishopric of Canterbury arrived, and in the first week of April, Parliament passed the bill Cromwell had masterminded, the Act in Restraint of Appeals, meaning that any verdict concerning the king's marriage could not be challenged in Rome. Mantel's Cromwell visits Katherine, still fighting her husband. Katherine can be as fierce as Anne, but she is not sharp; rather, she has the strength of her conviction, and as Cromwell marvels, she is unyielding:

She may smile, but she doesn't yield an inch. Julius Caesar would have had more compunction. Hannibal.

While Katherine stubbornly waited for a verdict from Rome, Archbishop Thomas Cranmer in his new role pronounced Henry to be divorced from his queen of 24 years, in a small trial at Dunstable Priory in Bedfordshire in

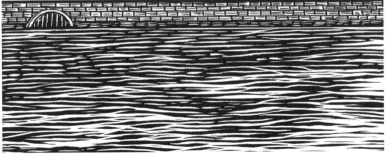

May. It was remarkably quick; Katherine was now relegated to the status of Princess Dowager. Anne's coronation was planned for the last days of June.

In *Wolf Hall*, 'he, Thomas Cromwell, is now running everything, including the weather'. London witnessed three days of glorious celebrations and the main event, the coronation on 1 June 1533, was magnificent – and likely exhausting for the six months pregnant Anne.

Mantel's Cromwell visits Chapuys, who has secluded himself in defiance of the coronation. Historically, though Chapuys found the whole thing in poor taste, he was out on the Thames, a guest at a banquet held on the German ambassador's barge where they drank a toast to the Emperor as the guns of the Tower fired. Not everyone approved, but no one was going to miss it.

PRINCE[ESS]

It was now a waiting game. The proclamations were carefully drawn up, ready to be sent to all the corners of Europe, to announce the birth of a prince, which would prove that God smiled on the King of England. The letters all confidently announced a prince, and in *Wolf Hall*, it is Cromwell who suggests the scribes leave a space at the end of 'prince': 'so if need be you can squash in ... But they look at him as if he's a traitor, so he leaves off.'

Of course, the baby Anne gave birth to on 7 September was not the long-awaited prince, but a princess. Henry and Anne rally and put on a brave face: they were still young, and surely sons would follow. Cromwell thinks very little of the newborn and in *The Mirror and the Light* even refers to her as the ginger pig, rather unkindly (not every child is Grace Cromwell). But Anne, seemingly softer, is infatuated with her daughter, longing to nurse her, which is not part of the royal custom: queens are there to breed, not feed.

PERSONAL SPHERES

Throughout the rest of 1533 and 1534 we see more of the Cromwell household, so different from our first introduction. Cromwell is wealthy, powerful and influential. Austin Friars and his house in Stepney continue to host friends and patrons. Though the ghosts linger, the living children we saw at the beginning of *Wolf Hall* are now grown up; they are adults with their own desires and ambitions.

Rafe Sadler

Cromwell would have known Sadler's father, Henry, during their time serving the Grey family, and from the age of seven, Sadler was placed in Cromwell's care as a ward. In the Cromwell household he was taught to read and write, not only in English but also in French, Latin and Greek. By the time he was 19, Sadler was one of Cromwell's right-hand men and served as his secretary – who better to have as a mentor?

Sadler is a constant character throughout the trilogy, and we witness the transition from a young boy to a gentleman. Sadler married Ellen Barre, Cromwell's young laundress, whose husband had run off to Ireland. Despite this minor issue, the couple married and Ellen bore him seven children. Historically, Sadler survived Cromwell's fall and enjoyed a highly successful career at court as a Privy Councillor and diplomat, but he was dedicated to his mentor's memory, much like Cromwell had been to Wolsey. He remained close to Richard and Gregory Cromwell throughout his life and actively worked against those he considered responsible for Cromwell's death, in particular Gardiner and Norfolk. It was also most likely Sadler who took possession of Holbein's famed portrait of Thomas Cromwell, ensuring its survival through the centuries.

Gregory Cromwell

Gregory is often dismissed as an unintelligent, naive young man who did not possess any of his father's intellectual or political brilliance, but MacCulloch argues that this myth stems from a miscalculation of his age. Most likely born in 1520, he was a young boy when he struggled with his studies, not a teenager. Cromwell was close to his son and was determined to provide him with a fine education, sending him to a Benedictine nunnery run by the Prioress Margaret Vernon before he was sent to Cambridge, where he would be tutored by various scholars. Gregory also became accomplished in physical pursuits, including jousting and hawking.

As a young man at court, Gregory was well liked and respected, with the Duke of Norfolk praising him as a 'wise quick piece', and three humanist scholars dedicated their works and translations to him. Gregory had been moulded into the ideal courtier and he would prove to be a credit to his father, though he would not follow in his father's political footsteps, preferring a quieter life away from court and its deadly politics.

RENAISSANCE

RENAISSANCE INFLUENCES

Renaissance thought and cultural expression were inspired by the revival of classical learning and the flowering of cultural expression. From the 14th to the 17th century, following the culturally conservative Medieval period, the rich flourishing of philosophy, science and the arts spawned the Humanist Movement, an ethical system that advanced the concept of the dignity, freedom and the value of human beings; a shift of emphasis from religious to secular expression.

This was at the heart of the Renaissance, which spread throughout Europe, reaching England during Henry VIII's reign. It was accompanied by an explosion of trade, exploration and diplomatic exchanges that reached from Europe to the Ottoman and Persian empires. The creation of the printing press by Johannes Gutenberg in 1440 revolutionized the dissemination of Renaissance ideals to educated Europeans. Monarchs strove to become a Renaissance Prince, accomplished in the arts and physical pursuits; popular literary themes centred on the art of being a Renaissance Man. The courts of Europe entertained some of the greatest names of the age, including Leonardo Da Vinci, Michelangelo, Niccolò Machiavelli and Desiderius Erasmus. Throughout his life, Cromwell would become acquainted with some of the voices of the period who helped shape Renaissance culture.

THOMAS WYATT

Thomas Wyatt, poet, courtier and ambassador, is arguably one of the most important voices of the English Renaissance, whose poetry marked the beginning of the sonnet tradition in England.

Born in 1503 in Kent, Wyatt was the son of a war hero – Sir Henry Wyatt had been an early supporter of Henry Tudor, and was held prisoner by Richard III and presumably tortured. Their family crest proudly featured a 'barnacle', an instrument of torture used during his imprisonment. His injuries are still apparent at the time of *Wolf Hall*:

'It is forty years, more, since the Tower, but his smashed-up jaw still stiffens and plagues him with pain.'

His son, Thomas Wyatt, followed in his father's footsteps and worked his way up at court, beginning with his appointment as Clerk of the King's Jewels. In 1525 he was made Esquire of the Body, and was well placed to be picked as an ambassador for foreign postings. But Wyatt is primarily known for his poetry, and his relationship with Anne Boleyn. Mantel's Wyatt is somewhat ambiguous when discussing the extent of his relationship with Anne, and while there are many historians who argue there is no evidence that Anne and Wyatt were lovers, several of Wyatt's poems suggest that he held unrequited feelings for her. Henry never quite took to Wyatt, but his skill as an ambassador was undeniable, so he was often sent on lengthy diplomatic missions to Spain, France and Italy.

In *Wolf Hall*, Henry Wyatt begs Cromwell to take his son under his wing, and to be a mentor and father figure to him. The real Cromwell was close to Wyatt, an ally and patron, and their relationship would span Cromwell's life. Cromwell is fond of the young man, often rescuing him from complicated situations, many of which were his own doing. Following Cromwell's execution Wyatt wrote an eloquent verse that laid bare his grief at losing someone he considered a friend and mentor.

For Mantel's Wyatt, 'nothing is ever clear, and no truth a single truth'. It is this Wyatt who plants a seed in Cromwell's mind, one of many: 'The worst of it is her hinting, her boasting almost, that she says no to me but yes to others –' Wyatt thinks nothing of it, but Cromwell files the information away. The real Wyatt, however, remained steadfastly loyal to the Boleyns, with whom he was close.

While Wyatt is best remembered for his poetry – influenced by Italian styles, drawing on various stanza forms and measures – he also wrote several biting satires on life at the Tudor court, portraying courtly life as an empty façade and its participants as lacking moral integrity, intent on enriching themselves and their families, often at the expense of others. Virtue was only a façade, marriage was merely to move up in the world, and it was every man for himself. Wyatt might not be too far off the mark at times, but his was not the only view of the courtier and courtly literature.

What did it take to be the ideal courtier throughout the courts of Europe? It was one of most popular subjects of Renaissance political writing – scholars such as Desiderius Erasmus, Niccolò Machiavelli, and Baldassare Castiglione wrote extensively on the theme.

BALDASSARE CASTIGLIONE

Baldassare Castiglione, the count of Casatico, a small town 50 miles (80km) north of Pisa, was an Italian courtier, diplomat, soldier and a prominent Renaissance scholar. His most famous work *Il Libro del Cortegiano* (The Book of the Courtier), was first published in Italy in 1528. In this he detailed his expert and experienced advice to fellow courtiers like himself and received considerable acclaim. The book was a series of fictional dialogues set in the ducal palace of Urbino, where, over the course of four evenings, the characters engage in a series of debates all focused on a courtier's life.

Reading Castiglione, it is not difficult not to catch glimpses of Cromwell: the ideal courtier was multi-faceted, at home with a sword and a quill, possessed knowledge of art and literature, and was crucially, 'of humble birth who, through their virtues, won glory for their descendants'.

Castiglione is mentioned briefly in *Wolf Hall*, with Henry and Cromwell discussing one of his main themes, the art of *sprezzatura*, which is:

'The art of doing everything gracefully and well, without the appearance of effort. A quality princes should cultivate, too.' He [Henry] *adds, rather dubious, 'King Francis has it.'*

Neither the fictional portrayal nor the historical Cromwell seemed to practice *sprezzatura* – the art of studied carelessness. However, we do know that he owned a copy of Castiglione's book, and might have been one of the first. Edmund Bonner, a chaplain in Wolsey's household and future Bishop of London, wrote to Cromwell in 1530, asking to loan 'the book called Cortegiano in Ytalian'. Bonner also desired to become more Italianicized so his future Italian embassies might be successful, and who better to teach him?

NICCOLÒ MACHIAVELLI

Cardinal Reginald Pole was the first to suggest that Cromwell had been influenced by Niccolò Machiavelli, the famed Florentine author, soldier, diplomat and philosopher, whose works, in Pole's view, bordered on the satanic. Machiavelli makes a minor appearance in *Wolf Hall*: it is 1527 and we learn that Cromwell:

... has got Niccolò Machiavelli's book, Principalities. *It is a Latin edition, shoddily printed in Naples, which seems to have passed through many hands.*

Mantel is suggesting Cromwell's talents and political acumen – that is deceit, realpolitik and cunning – must be because he had been influenced by Machiavelli's work. But we have to look at Pole's accusations which we find in his *Apologia Ad Carolum Quintum*, written in 1539, where Pole falsifies Cromwell's rise to power: he armed Cromwell with Machiavellian arguments and guile which misled the king on matters of religion.

Pole wrote that in 1528 he and Cromwell had discussions regarding the duty of a counsellor to his king, and maintained that Cromwell offered to lend him a copy of the infamous *Il Principe*. However, some historians argue that Cromwell would have more likely offered Pole Castiglione's book, *Il Cortegiano*, which we know he owned. While Machiavelli's book was written for rulers, Castiglione's book was a manual for courtiers; though there is no reason why a book intended for princes could not be read by or influence courtiers, or the nobility. The issue is more a question of timing. Pole's accusation is suspect primarily because he vehemently opposed Cromwell's strategic plan. Pole was desperate to show that Henry could never have devised such depraved measures: the break with Rome; the declaration of supremacy over the church; and the dissolution of the monasteries. Such deeds had to have been the work of the devil, at least influenced by a heretical doctrine, that of Machiavelli's *Il Principe*, all of which was Cromwell's doing. As it happened Pole's *Apologia*, printed in 1539, came at a time when Cromwell had launched a systematic attack on the Pole family who were suspected of engaging in treasonous behaviour and plotting against the king.

Pole clearly blamed Cromwell for leading Henry astray politically and religiously, and accused Cromwell of being a demon and a disciple of Machiavelli – it is not clear which was worse. But these are the historical details around the controversy. The outstanding issue is whether Cromwell could have read the book as early as 1527, the year Machiavelli died. *Il Principe* had not yet been printed in 1527: the first printed edition was in 1532, and the Latin edition was not available until the 1560s, long after Cromwell's death. In *The Mirror and the Light*, Mantel suggests Cromwell was familiar with Machiavelli's work prior to its publication, and that he even possessed a printed version – perhaps it was an illegal copy, possibly dictated by someone who had seen the original. Mantel also draws on correspondence between Cromwell and his friend Henry Parker, Lord Morley, Jane Rochford's father, who was a respected courtier and translator. Morley sent Cromwell a copy of Machiavelli's printed work in the late 1530s, and his letter suggests that Cromwell had not yet seen it. Surely Cromwell would have told the like-minded Morley that he had an unprinted version and shared it with him, for it was not deemed a heretical work in England. There is no historical evidence that shows Cromwell saw a copy of *Il Principle* in the 1520s, nor that Morley's edition was the first to pass into Cromwell's hands, but it is tempting to draw a line from Machiavelli's political brilliance to that of Cromwell.

Hans Holbein (the Younger)

I can, whenever I please, make seven lords of seven ploughmen, but I cannot make one Holbein of even seven Lords.
Henry VIII

There are many benchmarks to measure one's 'arrival' at court; one is when you sit for Mr Holbein to have your portrait painted. The German-born Holbein spent several years training in Basel before journeying to England in search of work in 1526. Armed with credentials from the great scholar Erasmus, he sought out Thomas More, who gave him his first commission, thus launching Holbein's career in England, where he spent most of his life. Holbein counted Cromwell among his patrons, as well as the Boleyns, for whom he designed jewellery and an exquisite cup for Anne complete with the falcon crest. By 1532 he was established as a royal painter, and his portraits for Henry VIII created the sense of majesty that exists today. He is responsible for some of the most iconic paintings of the period, including the now-lost Whitehall mural, *The Ambassadors*, and Cromwell's rather unflattering portrait. In 1534, Mantel's Cromwell appraises his face, forever inscrutable on canvas. In a conversation with his son he recalls that he once overheard a friend of George Boleyn's say he looked like a murderer; he

will proceed to ask everyone who views the portrait if they feel the same. Holbein would also paint the famous portrait of Anne of Cleves which so captivated Henry, but escaped any blame when Henry declared the portrait had deceived him. With the fall of Anne and Cromwell, Holbein lost two of his greatest benefactors, and returned to painting private commissions. He died in London, but his final resting place remains a mystery.

THE OATH OF SUCCESSION

Wolsey returns in 1534, a spectre shadowing Cromwell as he moves up in the world, speaking to his darkest fears:

Wolsey says, you know he will take the credit for your good ideas, and you the blame for his bad ones? When fortune turns against you, you will feel her lash: you always, he never.

Cromwell's ascendency continued, being confirmed as Principal Secretary and Chief Minister, positions which he had already occupied unofficially for some time.

March and April of 1534 continued apace as Cromwell secured Henry's first goal, the Act of Succession declaring Elizabeth legitimate and Mary illegitimate, which was passed by Parliament. Cromwell also visited Mary to inform her of her new status and her new position: she would now serve in the household of her half-sister, Elizabeth, whose very existence was the cause of her diminished status. Mantel's Mary is like a little doll, somewhat confused and disoriented, unable to grasp the dramas around her. However, the real Mary Tudor was far more feisty and understood every attempt of Henry's to weaken her status; she often sent Henry's councillors scurrying from her rooms. Although Mary and Katherine still had their loyal supporters, Henry was determined to expunge them from his new life.

The Act had a sting in its tail: all subjects, if required, must swear an oath recognizing the Act as well as the king's marriage to Anne Boleyn. Henry, Cromwell and Anne had two individuals in their sights whom this Act was designed to force into submission: Thomas More, who thus far had tried to keep out of the drama; and Bishop John Fisher, Katherine's staunch defender.

The day of reckoning came on 13 April, when More was summoned to appear before a commission, comprising Archbishop Cranmer, Thomas Cromwell, Lord Chancellor Audley and the Abbot of Westminster, William Benson, at Lambeth Palace, and swear his allegiance to the Act of Succession. While More was willing to accept Henry's marriage to Anne, he could not abide the new law of succession, which declared Mary a bastard. He was immediately sent to the Tower – decades of friendship extinguished in a mere matter of minutes.

The year 1534 became an *annus horribilis*. Not only were Henry and Anne struggling to cope with events domestically, they were then dealt a major blow as news reached England of Charles V's triumph over the Ottoman ruler, Suleiman the Magnificent, and his general Hayreddin Barbarossa, in the battle for Tunis as part of their constant struggle for supremacy in the region. As Francis I was Suleiman's ally at the time, a victorious Charles took the opportunity to force France into another alliance. Cromwell, Chapuys reported, was scarcely able to breathe when he heard the news. France now cooled towards Henry.

Events were already taking a toll on the royal marriage; the new queen is frustrated and agitated, Henry seems darker too. His enemies are closer to home: he is determined to destroy Thomas More and Bishop Fisher, despite Cromwell's reluctance. For the first time, Cromwell glimpses malice, a portent of things to come. Henry says:

'I keep you, Master Cromwell, because you are as cunning as a bag of serpents. But do not be a viper in my bosom. You know my decision. Execute it.'

Bishop Fisher and Thomas More were sentenced to execution for refusing to swear the Oath of Succession. Like More, Fisher was willing to swear allegiance to Henry and Anne's children, but they also refused to repudiate papal supremacy over the English church. The denial of the royal titles was, by 1535, treasonable, and Bishop Fisher was facing execution. In a clever attempt to protect Fisher, Pope Paul III, who had succeeded Clement VII in 1534, formally made Fisher a cardinal, wrongly assuming that Henry would hardly dare to execute him.

History tells us that Cromwell tried to save More by persuading him just to acquiesce and accept the oath: just say 'Yes'. *Wolf Hall* conjures conversations within the recesses of the Tower, relating frank discussions in which Mantel gives us a glimpse of a very human and vulnerable More, even if, like Cromwell, we cannot fathom a principle strong enough to die for.

Fisher was executed on 22nd June followed by More on 6th July 1535. More's last words were: 'I died a servant of the King's, but God's first.'

Cromwell has no time for sentimentality – life must go on – and he is already planning Henry's calendar for the last few weeks of summer, before the winter chill rolls in and Henry can no longer hunt:

'Now here, before we go to Winchester, we have time to spare, and what I think is, Rafe, we shall visit the Seymours.' He writes it down. Early September. Five days. Wolf Hall.

4
HENRY'S
WRATH

AROUND THE THRONE
THE THUNDER ROLLS

In *Bring Up the Bodies*, the summer of 1535 sees a despondent and depressed Henry as he faces disappointment and broken promises. Three years on, his marriage to Anne Boleyn has not produced a male heir, and the marriage is met with skepticism, in England and throughout Europe. There are no royal houses seeking a union with England through a marriage to the young Princess Elizabeth, whose legitimacy remains in doubt. Henry has little enthusiasm for his summer progress and travels with only a small selection of gentlemen, Cromwell included. None of Henry's visions have come to fruition; Katherine, rather than Anne, still held the hearts and minds of the English people, and the struggle to validate his second marriage was constant. There was hope – Anne was pregnant again, but by now Cromwell knew that a pregnancy guaranteed nothing.

The book opens with Henry's visit to Wolf Hall in 1535, the home of Sir John Seymour of 'Wulfhall', Wiltshire. Henry knows the family well but now suddenly notices the young Jane Seymour as if for the first time, although he has seen her many times at court.

Bring Up the Bodies also gives us a sense of Henry's advancing years:

... he looks bloated and puffy, and a vein is burst here and there, and even by candlelight you can see that his faded hair is greying.

Henry begins to cultivate the Seymours, his gracious hosts at Wolf Hall, Cromwell watching as Henry fawns over Jane. There is no one single moment when the reader can say with certainty that Cromwell's allegiance has shifted, but there is something about his choices which suggest a turning point. Relations between Anne and Cromwell have soured, he resents George Boleyn who treats him as an inferior, and he has little time for Thomas Boleyn; but he has unravelled Anne, and is seeing her in a different light.

... they are uneasy now, each of them vigilant, watching each other for some slip that will betray real feeling, and so give advantage to the one or the other: as if only dissimulation will make them safe.

Anne Boleyn was now around now thirty-four years old, and Mantel's Anne is still a skilful manipulator of men; it seems it is just Cromwell and now the king she is unable to please. Anne and Cromwell's alliance had always been a marriage of convenience and upon their return to court Mantel's Cromwell makes a snap decision: he tells Rafe to fetch Jane Seymour from Wolf Hall.

In the autumn of 1535, Mantel's Anne orders Cromwell up north: she and Henry have heard that Katherine is ill, but they want confirmation. Cromwell takes his leave but is accosted by Lady Worcester, one of Anne's ladies-in-waiting, who shares some tantalizing gossip. It is here Mantel plants some rather large seeds:

We all know where Harry Norris would like to lie tonight. Shelton is only his bedwarmer for now. He has royal ambitions. He will tell anyone. He is sick with love for the queen.

THE DEATH OF KATHERINE

Historically, we cannot know with certainty what Cromwell was thinking at the turn of the year. After all, Anne was pregnant, and whatever clashes she and Henry had, so far they had always come back together. But crucially, in January 1536, word reached court that Katherine, who had been exiled and separated from her daughter for years, was close to death.

Mantel's Cromwell visits her at Kimbolton, Cambridgeshire, noting that she is indeed ill, but instead of a sense of anticipation, he feels empathy:

... perhaps she dreams of the gardens of the Alhambra, where she grew up: the marble pavements, the bubbling of crystal water into basins, the drag of a white peacock's tail and the scent of lemons.

The meeting Mantel describes is poignant. Cromwell is respectful and frank, but he does not shy from the truth. Katherine is dying, and he wants her to save her daughter by reconciling with the king. Mantel sees the futility of Katherine's fearless determination, and utter hope, that she and her daughter will stand united and that Henry will yield to them. Historically, it was Chapuys who tried to advise Mary and balance Katherine's influence. Chapuys wanted to protect Mary at all costs, a sentiment that Mantel apportions to Cromwell. An anxious Chapuys begged Cromwell for permission to visit Katherine, but he was delayed a day as Henry wanted to see him before his departure, a scene which Mantel stages. The informal audience with Henry only serves to irritate him further: Chapuys is greeted with a bear hug from the exuberant king, who has heard Katherine is on her deathbed and can hardly contain his excitement.

As it happened, Chapuys would reach Katherine in time and was able to spend several days consoling her, assuring her; a devoted servant to the end. Katherine was heartened and seemed to rally so Chapuys returned to London, but on 8th January he is overtaken by news of her death and returned to a jubilant court. In many historical and fictional accounts, Thomas and George Boleyn remark loudly that it was a pity Mary had not joined her mother, but Chapuys, who wrote the dispatch, actually reported that the men must have said such a thing to themselves – an assumed sentiment, rather than a remark.

Jousts and tournaments were planned to celebrate not only Katherine's death, but also Anne's pregnancy. But that afternoon, at the jousts at Greenwich, the king was thrown from his horse, which reared and then fell on top of him. Henry lay unconscious for two hours. The court was thrown into complete chaos, described in *Bring Up the Bodies* – an hysterical Norfolk rushing at Cromwell: '"By God, Cromwell!" he snarls.' Cromwell has a moment of realization:

'How many men can say, as I must, "I am a man whose only friend is the King of England"? I have everything, you would think. And yet take Henry away and I have nothing.'

All believe Henry is dead, except Cromwell who sees he is breathing, but he is shaken. The news of Henry's fall and the initial belief that he has died is delivered with little tact by Norfolk to his niece, Anne, who is genuinely distraught. Five days later, the day Katherine is buried, Anne miscarries a boy. Cromwell knows that Henry now wants to be rid of Anne, and curiously, Katherine's death has paved the way. Henry could hardly be rid of his second queen while his first was still living. Cromwell spends the next weeks in conference with the Seymours, coaching Jane on how she is now to behave with the king, grooming her. The stakes have been raised, and marriage may well be on the table. Jane is the antithesis of Anne, and the dutiful Cromwell makes sure everyone sees the contrast:

Notice how he speaks of Jane: so humble, so shy. Even Archbishop Cranmer must recognise the portrait, the black reverse portrait of the present queen.

THE FALL OF THE BOLEYNS

In his seven years at court, Chapuys had never met Anne, so it was of great interest to everyone attending Easter Mass of 1536 how they would react when they inevitably crossed paths. It is a great moment in history and Mantel has her take on it:

Anne turns her head. A pointed smile: and to the enemy, she makes a reverence, a gracious inclination of her jewelled neck. Chapuys screws up his eyes tight, and bows to the concubine.

Mantel's Chapuys worries about how the Emperor will react when the exchange is reported to him, but this is not quite what happened. We know that it was Chapuys who first bowed to Anne as she walked past, and what surprised him was Anne's reaction: 'I must say that she was affable enough on the occasion for on my being placed behind the door by which she entered the chapel, she turned round to return the reverence which I made her when she passed.'

We do not know exactly why Anne did this, but it is possible that, with Katherine gone and the French clearly no longer willing to be allies, Anne had been advised to show some favour to Chapuys, but more importantly, through him she would show respect to Charles V. In *Bring Up the Bodies*, the explanation is simpler: Henry has forced Chapuys to acknowledge his second marriage:

... to a queen whom he no longer wants. ... Now, if he likes, he can let it go.

Cromwell has filed away all the rumours, all the snide comments and tidbits fed to him over the years about Anne. He sits at his desk and shakes them all out, laying them in front of him. He has names: Henry Norris, Mark Smeaton, Francis Weston, William Brereton and George Boleyn.

In *Bring Up the Bodies*, Cromwell meets privately with Thomas and George Boleyn, flatly telling them that Anne is finished, and will likely be sent to a nunnery. Thomas seems to understand and accept the situation, while George bristles and refuses. Historically, no one saw Cromwell coming.

The subject of Anne's downfall is something of a crowded field – every historian and historical fiction author has their theory, resulting in a multitude of demises. That Anne and her co-accused were innocent cannot be disputed, for it was clearly an engineered downfall, but the truth of the plot and who was behind the machinations is almost impossible to determine. Certainly, the real Thomas Cromwell seems a likely suspect, but what we may never know is whether he acted against her of his own accord, or on the orders of Henry VIII. We do know that throughout 1536, Anne and Cromwell quarrelled on several occasions, with Anne threatening Cromwell that she would like to see 'his head off his shoulders'.

Mantel follows the trail of evidence, from Henry's accident through Anne's spats with Cromwell, and into April 1536. On Passion Sunday Anne's chaplain John Skip delivered an extraordinary sermon, declaring that the king needed to resist evil counsellors who tempted him to ignoble actions, and using the story of the Hamman, advisor to the Persian king Xerxes and an enemy of his wife, Esther. The lengthy allegory ended with Hamman being executed. No one failed to make the link.

There are other events to consider, namely Cromwell and Chapuys' ambitions for a rapprochement between Henry and Charles V, now that Katherine was no longer a sticking point. On Easter Monday, Cromwell met Henry, arriving at court before the king was even awake, so eager was he to report his meeting with Chapuys and the letters from Charles. Henry was receptive and pleased by Charles' words and looked forward to healing the rift between the two. It seemed as if an Imperial alliance was a real possibility, but while Henry had been receptive earlier that day, by the evening his mind had changed entirely.

Cromwell, who had worked hard for Imperial peace, was accused of making his own policy, in cahoots with Chapuys. Henry railed at both men so violently that they both made quick exits.

Mantel draws on Chapuys' own report, in which he ponders whether it was Anne who poisoned Henry against the proposal of peace. Chapuys adds that

Cromwell disappears for several days, sick from fear, or regrouping. Mantel imagines the conversation between Henry and Cromwell before the latter departs, making it clear who she believes set things in motion:

He is here to take instructions. Get me Jane: Jane, so kind, who sighs across the palate like sweet butter. Deliver me from bitterness, from gall.

GATHERING EVIDENCE

Cromwell invites Elizabeth Somerset, Countess of Worcester, to a meeting. A lady-in-waiting of the queen's, she is in a difficult situation, pregnant with a child who was not her husband's. Historically, we know that Elizabeth becomes involved when she is chastised by her brother, courtier Sir Anthony Browne, for her loose living, and she retorts that her behaviour is nothing compared to that of the queen. She would turn out to be one of the main witnesses against Anne, but Mantel has changed the narrative slightly. Meeting with Cromwell, Elizabeth voices the same defence and starts a revolution, with the women of Anne's bedchamber clamouring over each other to accuse the queen of immoral behaviour with her male courtiers. We do know that several of Anne's ladies would bear witness against her, but not necessarily their motives. But one name appears more often in the narrative of the Boleyns' downfall than any other: Jane, George Boleyn's wife.

Jane Rochford is a malevolent character in the trilogy, unhappily married, and a disgruntled member of the Boleyn family. She seems loyal but is also triumphant when any member of the family suffers humiliation. She whispers poison in Cromwell's ear about Anne and the Boleyns – at first Cromwell recognizes that she is lonely and 'breeding a savage heart', but throughout the years he appreciates the intelligence, and will use it. Surprisingly, some of Cromwell's lengthiest interactions in the trilogy are with her, though theirs is a curious relationship based on the currency of information.

JANE ROCHFORD

Like the Boleyns, Jane hailed from Norfolk, the daughter of Henry Parker, Lord Morley, a well-respected translator, ambassador and member of the Privy Council. Jane first entered Katherine of Aragon's household as a lady-in-waiting, and, in 1524, her father began negotiations with the Boleyn family for a match between Jane and George Boleyn. Jane's older sister, Margaret, had married one of Thomas Boleyn's nephews, John Shelton, which had been a successful alliance between the two families. In almost all fictional portrayals, the marriage seems to have been forced on two unwilling participants and it is popular to portray George as verbally and even physically abusive towards his wife, but there is no evidence to suggest George and Jane were miserable throughout their marriage. Mantel draws on the traditional portrayal of Jane, who takes a perverse pleasure in sowing doubt in Anne's mind and deliberately provoking her, and has no qualms sharing with Cromwell what goes on in Anne's chambers.

Mantel has Jane suggesting what would become the extraordinary charge of incest, telling Cromwell that Anne and George are lovers. Of course there is no evidence of such an accusation, in fact it seems to have stemmed from Elizabeth Somerset. George was too powerful to be allowed to survive; the charge may well say more about Cromwell than anyone else.

Jane is usually instrumental in Anne and George's downfall in the fictional portrayals, though she makes no appearance in any of the extant records, nor is she listed as giving evidence. Jane has become a scapegoat, unfairly vilified. But in Mantel's series, she keeps the intrigue bubbling along and advises Cromwell to where to begin.

An Invitation

The real Mark Smeaton was a Flemish musician within Anne's household, and there is no evidence he and Cromwell knew each other in any way. Mantel, however, has linked their narratives, placing Smeaton in Cardinal Wolsey's household, an arrogant young man who mocks the Cardinal's downfall and treats Cromwell as an inferior.

We know that Cromwell invited Smeaton to his house in Stepney to be interrogated, with many historians suggesting the musician was tortured to confess to having an affair with Anne. No reliable contemporary accounts state that Smeaton was tortured and he seemed in good health on the scaffold, as much as one can be. Mantel clearly does not believe the allegation of torture, and has Cromwell coax Smeaton into a boastful confession, naming two other men as rivals – Francis Weston and Henry Norris – which he immediately regrets:

Five rash minutes of boasting, in one ungratified life and, like nervous tradesmen, the gods at once send in their account.

Smeaton admitted to having had sex with the queen and sources tell us that Cromwell wrote at once to the king outlining 'Smeaton's confession'.

Despite (or due to) the machinations moving below the surface, Henry decided to proceed with the May Day jousts, presided over by Anne Boleyn in her last public display as queen. But Henry's eye was on Henry Norris, his Groom of the Stool. We know that in the middle of the tournament, Henry left abruptly, taking Henry Norris with him. Norris was accused of intercourse with the queen, which he indignantly refused. He was dropped off at the Tower and it is enough to bring Anne in herself.

Anne was at Greenwich watching a tennis tournament on 2nd May when she received instructions to meet with the Privy Council. Anne stood before her uncle Norfolk, Sir William FitzWilliam and Sir William Paulet, who outlined charges of adultery with three men, for which she would be taken to the Tower. Anne was kept in her apartments until the Thames tide became favourable, and at two o'clock in the afternoon she stepped onto the royal barge and was rowed up the river to the Tower, likely entering via the Court Gate near the Byward Tower – the usual entrance for nobility and royalty, rather than Traitor's Gate. We know from William Kingston, the Constable of the Tower, that upon entering the Tower, Anne was informed she would be lodged in those familiar queen's apartments, whereupon she broke down into hysterical tears and declared that it was too good for her. This has sometimes been taken as evidence of a degree of guilt, but Mantel's Cromwell feels he knows what she means:

When she said the queen's lodgings were too good for her, she did not mean to admit her guilt, but to say this truth: I am not worthy, and I am not worthy because I have failed.

Historically, one of Anne's main concerns while at the Tower was for her family, asking after her parents, worrying that her fate, and that of her brother, would kill their mother, and worrying for George. As we see in *The Mirror and the Light*, George, brought in the same day as Anne, was mostly concerned for those who might suffer as a result of his death; indeed he was so distressed that Sir William Kingston wrote to Cromwell on his behalf to ask for help.

The other men are brought to the Tower with Francis Weston being admitted last on 5th May. Thomas and Elizabeth Boleyn did not visit Anne and George, a fact which is used as evidence of their ruthless callousness towards their children, but more than likely, they were forbidden to visit, obliged to remain silent.

INTERROGATION

So much of the documentation pertaining to Anne's arrest has vanished, and Cromwell's interrogations of the four men can only be guessed at, but the interrogations which Mantel has conjured are punctuated by one linking theme: left forepaw, right forepaw, right hindpaw and left hindpaw. Four positions, four men. The devils who tormented the cardinal in the masque.

Cromwell first questions Norris, where flirtatious banter between himself and the queen is placed before him, twisted into something far more licentious. Norris would be accused of having intercourse with the queen on 6th and 31st October 1533 at Westminster. The usually meticulous Cromwell should have checked those dates: Anne was actually at Greenwich, recovering from childbirth. Not that it mattered at this stage.

For Brereton's interrogation, Mantel's Cromwell does not even bother to discuss the charges, but rather what he feels Brereton is guilty of, referencing Brereton's covering up of a murder committed by his servants. In reality, it is more likely that Brereton's opposition to Cromwell's administrative reforms, particularly in Wales, led to his removal. When George Boleyn is examined, we get a sense that Mantel's Cromwell does not believe the charges of incest, but he does believe George to be an arrogant man who has no morals or religious conviction – a belief which does not do George justice.

Weston, of all the men, understands that it is not just about Wolsey, but his own treatment of Cromwell over the years, and apologizes, but Mantel has Weston on the precipice of admitting something. Rather than waiting for the man to speak, Cromwell leaves the room. This is perhaps Mantel's way of excusing her man; avoiding the pronouncement of a historical verdict either way. Mantel does not want to tell us either that Anne is guilty or that she is innocent.

Throughout these interrogations, it is clear that we are being invited to follow Cromwell's logic but we are being asked, without judgement, to understand Cromwell's rationale:

He needs guilty men. So he has found men who are guilty. Though perhaps not guilty as charged.

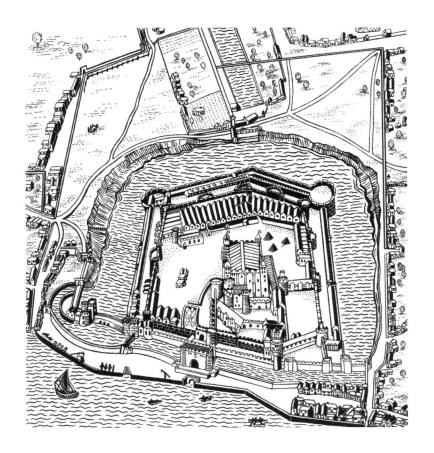

Then it is Anne's turn. Without evidence, we can only imagine Cromwell's examination of his former ally, and again, Anne's true guilt is somewhat ambiguous. We believe Mantel's Anne when she is emotional, irrational, uncomprehending of how her life has collapsed around her, and she appeals to Cromwell who, just for a moment, hesitates:

But then she raises her hands and clasps them at her breast, in the gesture Lady Rochford had showed him. Ah, Queen Esther, he thinks. She is not innocent; she can only mimic innocence.

Of course, Cromwell does not say she is guilty.

TRIAL AND EXECUTION

Cromwell engineered the trial of Anne and her co-accused, ensuring that there could be no other outcome but a guilty charge, supplied by a jury openly against Anne Boleyn. The trial threatened to erupt into chaos, with Cromwell barely managing to keep a hold on events. Even the day before the trial, Norfolk, who would preside over events, was still asking what the charges actually were – Cromwell was still working this out.

The men, excluding George who would be tried separately as a peer, were tried on 14 May. All were found guilty, which meant that Anne and George's convictions were a forgone conclusion.

Mantel's Cromwell watches Anne as she is tried, he marvels that she doesn't seem to believe it all. This Anne is impassive and seems to be a world away, but historical accounts of Anne's trial suggests she was composed and dignified, calmly refuting all of the charges. Regardless of the facts, both she and George were convicted of high treason and sentenced to death.

Henry allows Anne a small mercy: she will be beheaded not with an axe but a French sword, wielded by a French swordsman from Calais. Mantel points out one important fact, denoting the contrived nature of Anne's downfall – Henry is no innocent cuckold. In *Bringing Up the Bodies* Jean de Dinteville, a French diplomat, shares this news with Cromwell and Sir William Kingston. Cromwell wants to make sure Kingston has understood:

'Did you get that?' he asks. 'Henry has sent to Calais for the headsman.'
'By the Mass,' Kingston says. 'Did he do it before the trial?'
'So monsieur the ambassador tells me.'

17 May 1536

Cromwell is neither present historically, nor on the page, as George, Weston, Brereton, Smeaton and Norris are executed. Records of George's eloquent speech have survived the centuries:

And if I have offended any man that is not here now, either in thought, word or deed, and if ye hear any such, I pray you heartily in my behalf, pray them to forgive me for God's sake... I say unto you all, that if I had followed God's word in deed as I did read it and set it forth to my power, I had not come to this. If I had, I had been a living man among you.

19 May 1536

Historical records follow Anne's last hours in the Tower, as she prays and swears on the sacrament of her innocence. Mantel's Cromwell stands on the scaffold, testing the wooden beams.

Before 9am, Sir William Kingston led Anne and four maidservants out to the scaffold, and it was reported that Anne 'went to her execution with an untroubled countenance'. There was a scaffold but no block, since Anne was to be decapitated by a French swordsman, and would kneel upright for the blow. Mantel's Cromwell can barely hear Anne's last words: they come on the wind, fragmented. Thankfully, we have some records of her final speech:

Good Christian people, I am come hither to die, according to law, for by the law I am judged to die, and therefore I will speak nothing against it. I come here only to die, and thus to yield myself humbly to the will of the King, my lord. ... Thus I take my leave of the world, and of you, and I heartily desire you all to pray for me. Oh, Lord, have mercy on me. To God I commend my soul.

Mantel describes the moment:

Then a silence, and into that silence, a sharp sigh or a sound like a whistle through a keyhole: the body exsanguinates, and its flat little presence becomes a puddle of gore.

We might imagine a flurry of activity as Anne's body was hastily packed away, but Anne's body lay on the scaffold for a few hours after her execution because no one was prepared. Her head and body were placed in an empty arrow chest and brought to the chapel of St Peter ad Vincula, at the Tower, and interred under the altar.

We do not know what else Cromwell did that day, whether he returned to his desk, thinking no more of his vanquished enemies, or whether, as Mantel has it, he sits with a friend and reflects on the bloodshed. But Mantel has captured Cromwell's unwavering, unapologetic stance.

Once you have chosen a course, you should not apologise for it. God knows, I mean nothing but good to our master the king. I am bound to obey and serve. And if you watch me closely you will see me do it.'

When Cromwell asks Wriothesley to 'drink my health', he is not just inviting us to make a toast – we are seeing the celebration of a new era, a new queen, new court favourites, many of whom owe their positions to him.

AFTER THE EXECUTION

In the opening scene of *The Mirror and the Light* Anne Boleyn's head lies on the scaffold, a few feet from her bloodied, exposed neck. George and his co-accused have been interred in the chapel in the Tower of London. Having symbolically devoured his enemies, Cromwell fancies a second breakfast.

Historians have long debated the reasons why Cromwell moved so decisively against Anne as, for so many years, they had been regarded as allies. However, apart from a mutual interest in religious reform, there is no evidence that they were ever close. Mantel's Anne may have laughingly called Cromwell 'her man', but historically Anne was not responsible for any of Cromwell's favours or advancement, nor did she promote any of his friends, family members or close associates. Cromwell may have kept his distance because, as his biographer Diarmaid MacCulloch writes, he could neither forget nor forgive what he believed to be her part in the downfall of his mentor, Cardinal Wolsey. Equally, Anne would have done likewise, for she could never forget that Wolsey was Cromwell's first master, and therefore Cromwell was not to be entirely trusted.

But, of course, Cromwell did not act alone against Anne – certainly the entire game plan had Henry's consent – and there were a multitude of circumstances that led to her execution. While Katherine had brought the power and prestige of the Holy Roman Empire to the court of Henry VIII, Anne had brought nothing. It had been a costly gamble for Henry that yielded no reward. Cromwell served Henry, not Anne. This was not a personal betrayal, it was business. Cromwell simply came out on top.

The Mirror and the Light begins where *Bring Up the Bodies* ends: Cromwell is looking up at the scaffold where Anne had knelt moments before; he turns around and walks away, his son and the Duke of Suffolk alongside him. There are no letters or accounts by Cromwell that might indicate what he truly felt about Anne's death, but we do have Chapuys' reports to Charles V. One, in particular, informs Charles that some weeks following Anne's execution Chapuys had an illuminating conversation with Cromwell, some of which has found its way into *The Mirror and the Light*:

'I was not responsible for Anne's death,' he says. 'She herself brought it about, she and her gentlemen.'"
'But at a time of your choosing.'

The real Chapuy's reports reveal that Cromwell was quite forthcoming, keen to assure Chapuys that with Anne's death their diplomatic negotiations would run smoother; he confided that he had masterminded Anne's downfall, but only because Henry had authorized and commissioned him to prosecute Anne quickly in order to have her taken care of. As Mantel's Jane Seymour notes with sharp clarity, 'The king never does an unpleasant thing. Lord Cromwell does it for him.' There is no historical evidence to indicate that Cromwell ever regretted this entire episode and his role in its conclusion: whereas Mantel's Cromwell seems haunted by Anne's execution, and the innocent men executed alongside her.

Henry, however, was determined to erase every memory of her, particularly those he could see. He insisted that the hundreds of carved and painted examples of their intertwined initials be removed from every inch of his domain, just as he had done with the emblems from his previous marriage. Throughout the book, Mantel has Cromwell and others at court notice instances of carvings that have survived the purge; some even exist today, such as the one in the Great Hall at Hampton Court Palace: 'Shelton!' the duke yells. 'You've got a HA-HA. Knock it out, man. Do it while the weather's fine'.

We know that as soon as Henry heard of Anne's execution, he rushed to be with Jane Seymour and her family. The following day they were betrothed and eleven days later they were married in the Queen's Closet at Whitehall by Bishop Gardiner, now back in favour with Henry. In fact, much would change: with the Boleyns obliterated, there was a clean sweep of the Privy Chamber and the court, allowing new families to rise to positions of power and influence. The Cromwell family was one of them.

PERSONAL SPHERES

In *The Mirror and the Light*, Cromwell is at the very height of his power and his life reflects the influence he enjoyed. In July 1536 he succeeded Anne's father, Thomas Boleyn as Lord Privy Seal, and he is one of the most powerful men at court. At the gates of Austin Friars, crowds of petitioners shout his name in the hope of gaining his attention and having their papers read. His London residence bears witness to the comings and goings of those closest to Cromwell: Rafe, Richard Cromwell and Gregory frequent its halls. Rafe has risen in Henry's esteem – he has been appointed as Gentleman of the Privy Chamber, perfectly placed to be Cromwell's eyes and ears in the inner sanctum. The king has become increasingly fond of Rafe, granting him rewards that would continue for the rest of his reign, and would result in Rafe being one of the richest commoners in the country. In *The Mirror and the Light*, Gregory has grown from the gentle teenager with no sense for Latin to a man whose company is widely sought: 'From Somerset to Kent, from the midlands to the northern fells, castles and manors compete to entertain him.' Cromwell's nephew, Richard, is his uncle's trusted agent and always at his side. These three young men are a constant presence in the household despite their separate lives and duties. As Mantel's Cromwell surveys his dynasty, he reflects: 'he has trained them, encouraged them, written them as versions of himself'.

Another welcome guest at Austin Friars is Thomas Wriothesley (see chapter 3), a frequent addition to the Cromwell household, and Richard Rich, a protégé of Thomas Audley who worked with Cromwell over the years. Throughout the early 1530s, Rich benefitted from his relationship with both Audley and Cromwell as he began to audit monasteries around the country. Rich had also been close to Thomas More as a boy, and yet played a significant role in his trial for treason. Cromwell would have done well to take note of Rich's flexibility when it came to allegiances.

Cromwell also attempts to connect with his daughter, Janneke, alongside Dorothea, Wolsey's illegitimate daughter. Janneke remains aloof, whereas Dorothea despises Cromwell, believing he betrayed her father, an accusation which strikes at the very heart of Cromwell's being. Wolsey, who had been such a reassuring physical and spectral presence in the first two books, is all but silent in *The Mirror and the Light*, as if Cromwell's memory of his beloved master has been corrupted and he can no longer conjure him.

THE NEW COURT STRUCTURE

Along with the Cromwell supporters, conservative factions who had assisted Cromwell in bringing down Anne and her faction now step onto centre stage as we are introduced to new families, new alliances and new rivalries.

THE SEYMOURS

The Seymours could trace their origins back to the Norman invasion of 1066. Their original name, St Maur, likely hailed from the village of St-Maur-sur-Loire in Touraine. For several centuries they remained small landowners, and apart from the odd knighthood, were not considered to be part of the country gentry.

Fortunes changed with the marriage of Roger Seymour and Matilda or Maud, daughter and sole heir of William Esturmy, sometime in 1405. The Esturmy family had been the wardens of Savernake Forest in Wiltshire since the Norman invasion, an honour which passed down the generations. Savernake remains the only ancient forest in Britain which is still privately owned. The Esturmy family owned a modest estate in the middle of the forest which appears in the Domesday book with the Saxon name 'Ulfela'. Ulf Hall, Wulfhall or Wolf Hall became the premier estate of the Seymour family.

It was not until the early 16th century that family fortunes improved significantly, with the marriage in 1494 of John Seymour and Margaret (or Margery) Wentworth, first cousin of a familiar – and prolific – generation of Howards, namely Thomas Howard, Duke of Norfolk, his sister Elizabeth, mother of Anne Boleyn, and Edmund, father of Henry's fifth queen, Catherine Howard.

Wolf Hall is the setting for a pivotal moment in the course of English history when Henry VIII and Anne Boleyn are guests of Sir John Seymour in the last days of the summer progress of 1535. Wolf Hall was a large half-timbered manor surrounded by almost 1300 acres of lush parkland, boasting a long gallery, courtyard, broad chamber, and a chapel, surrounded by three gardens. The family would eventually abandon Wolf Hall for the grander estate of Tottenham House, and by 1571 it had fallen into disrepair.

Our introduction to the Seymours involves a surprisingly salacious bit of gossip, as Anne Boleyn gleefully tells Cromwell of a scandal at Wolf Hall: Sir John Seymour has been having an illicit affair with his son Edward's wife, Catherine. The theory has endured because it is so diverting, but the evidence is flimsy. 17th-century ecclesiastical author Peter Hely wrote that Edward Seymour had been taught magic while he was in France in 1527, which he used to spy on his wife back in England, catching her with a mysterious gentleman. Another 17th-century source alleges that she 'was known by his father after the wedding'. Catherine had clearly displeased her family as she is excluded from her father's will and was only given a small stipend of £40 on the condition that she retired to a convent. The 'scandal' continues throughout *Wolf Hall*, but it is curious that Henry would have married a woman whose family reputation was so tainted, unless, of course, it wasn't quite so simple.

JANE AND HER SIBLINGS

Historians have since pondered how Jane Seymour not only captured Henry's attention but then held it long enough to be elevated to Queen Consort. It certainly baffled her contemporaries, with various ambassadors including Chapuys writing to their respective masters that she must possess some special quality which only Henry could see.

Mantel's Cromwell is always interested in Jane's circumstances, taking pity on her during her family's scandal, presenting her with dainty gifts to cheer her up. He is quite drawn to Jane and even entertains romantic notions, which are destined to be thwarted. Jane serves as lady-in-waiting to both Katherine and Anne, although Mantel suggests Jane had more than one role at court, possibly as a spy.

Our evidence is scant regarding Jane's formative years, but we do know that she was one of ten children, and was born at Wolf Hall in around 1508. Six of the children lived to adulthood: Jane, her two younger sisters, Elizabeth and Dorothy, and three elder brothers, Edward, Henry and Thomas. The Seymours did not enjoy any particular prominence, but the children received a good education befitting the family of a 16th-century gentleman. Jane was betrothed to William Dormer, son of Sir Robert and Lady Jane Dormer, a match brokered by Jane's cousin, Francis Bryan. The engagement was broken off by the Dormers because rumour had it that they considered the Seymours' social status did not benefit the family. But John Seymour was able to use his familial connection to the Howard family to secure two places for Jane and her sister Elizabeth (Bess) as ladies-in-waiting to Katherine of Aragon. Jane left court after Katherine fell from favour, but returned in 1535 to serve the new queen, Anne Boleyn.

Throughout this trilogy, Cromwell finds himself rather enamoured with both women at different times. Bess is described as an elegant woman, highly intelligent, witty and worldly. She married Sir Anthony Ughtred, Governor of Jersey, in 1530, who died four years later. The widowed Bess Seymour was clearly a desirable bride, and continued to attract attention, and from her letters, in particular to Cromwell, we catch a glimpse of a bold young woman who wrote with a frankness that the real Cromwell likely appreciated.

In *Bring Up the Bodies*, Chapuys admits to Cromwell that he cannot see Jane's appeal. When Chapuys asks Cromwell what Henry sees in Jane, Cromwell answers simply: 'He thinks she's stupid. He finds it restful.' Henry and Jane's courtship played out before the entire court and beyond – everyone awaited the next instalment of Henry's domestic arrangements.

As Jane's star ascends, we begin to see more of Jane's brothers, Edward and Thomas, in the sources and in Mantel's series. They have flitted in and out of the narrative thus far, and now Cromwell feels it wise to nurture a closer relationship. But it is not all politics. Mantel's Cromwell sees two very different personalities: Edward, the eldest of the Seymour siblings, enjoyed a modest career at court. He served in Charles Brandon's French campaign of 1523, for which he was awarded a knighthood. In 1525, Edward was appointed Master of the Horse to Henry's illegitimate son Henry Fitzroy, before entering Cardinal Wolsey's household, where he may well have met Cromwell. In 1531, Edward was made an Esquire of the Body to the king, sealing his role at court. Edward was handsome, athletic, but serious and scholarly. Wolsey liked him, and Mantel's Cromwell finds him to be reliable. Thomas Seymour, on the other hand, would not experience the same stellar rise to prominence, often overshadowed by his brother. His time would come after Cromwell's death, and thus to Cromwell he is mostly just handsome.

THE RISE OF THE SEYMOURS

The year 1535 was a momentous one for the Seymours. Jane continued in Anne's household as lady-in-waiting, and hosted the royal couple at Wolf Hall on their summer progress. Within months, Henry's intentions towards Jane became evident. He was deeply smitten and a faction quickly formed around her, like bees around their queen. Apart from her immediate family, an important ally was Sir Nicholas Carew, Anne Boleyn's cousin, who did not share Anne's religious views and actively agitated against her, all the while tutoring Jane in how to keep the king's interest. Two other significant supporters were Francis Bryan, and, of course, Cromwell. The court watched as Henry wooed another lady-in-waiting in full view of his wife and

ministers. While the king had considerable experience of such affairs, it is difficult to get a sense of Jane during this hasty courtship. Historians have used and perpetuated the contrast between Anne and Jane – striking, dark-haired, intelligent and passionate versus bland, pale, weak-chinned and shy – to explain why Henry may have made such a choice. The despatches of Imperial Ambassador Eustace Chapuys are the source of detail about Anne Boleyn, but his communications from December 1536 through to November 1537 have disappeared from the archives, or perhaps they were destroyed, which means there is a lengthy gap in Chapuys' reports, depriving us of his rich and rewarding perspectives of this period, and of Henry's new queen.

Jane Rochford, returned to court in *The Mirror And The Light*, intimates to Cromwell that Jane is not as innocent as she appears, suggesting that she promoted friction and discord around her mistress, Anne Boleyn. Here, Mantel has Jane Rochford presenting the view of many historians who believe that, far from innocent, Jane and her faction contrived to present to the king a calm, rational and dignified foil to Anne's increasingly irrational temper and hysteria. The Seymours actively plotted against Anne, and one example of the strategies they employed is the rather hasty change to their family crest, which was originally a peacock's head and neck, its wings in mid-flight. But a humble woman like Jane could hardly have a proud peacock as her crest – the badge had to reflect the portrayal of Jane as meek and submissive. With a few brushstrokes, the peacock was transformed into a phoenix, the symbol of self-sacrifice.

Throughout the first months of 1536, Jane was coached carefully by her cousin, Nicholas Carew, and Cromwell may well have also played a part in instructing her. On one occasion, often recounted, Henry sent Jane a purse full of coins with a love letter, with the intention of making clear his intentions. Jane was likely forewarned and advised to make a rather theatrical display of the virtuous woman: she was careful not to open the letter but kissed it chastely, and then returned it unopened, begging the messenger to relay to the king that he might gift her when she had made an honourable match. It was a diplomatic way of extricating herself from a delicate situation: being propositioned by the king and spurning his advances.

Though Anne was never particularly popular, Jane was also not well-loved by the people to begin with. Many found Henry's haste to take a new wife, while Anne's head was still lying on the scaffold, objectionable. However, her deference and desire to reconcile Henry with his oldest child, Mary, and her appeal to Henry's gentler nature, endeared her to many and demonstrated a kindness and generosity of spirit that many felt Anne had lacked.

OLD FAMILIES, NEW ORDER

The Tudor period marked the shift from medieval to early modern. The reign of Henry VII changed the centuries-old power dynamic of the king and his people; he was unable to trust the ancient, powerful and conservative families that had always dominated the country. His 14-year-long exile informed his view of ableness and aptitude in the people around him. He chose new courtiers and new advisors – new men to serve under his rule and to heal the war-torn country. Skill now trumped lineage. When Henry VIII came to the throne, his challenges tested even the most devoted of the conservatives: he had the best of the new men to serve his will, and a formidable one it proved to be. Henry's subjects were required to support his marital and religious exploits: the usurpation of an anointed queen; the execution of two queen consorts; the king becoming Supreme Head of the Church in England; the execution of John Fisher, the Bishop of Rochester; the repudiation of the legitimacy of both of his daughters; and the execution of some of his most loyal subjects.

Anne Boleyn's reign had turned the country on its head, or in Wyatt's words, 'set the country in a roar' but the accession of Jane Seymour, it was hoped, heralded a return to the first golden years of Henry's reign, and if it didn't, the old families were prepared to replace the king in order to facilitate the matter.

THE POLES

The Pole family came from modest beginnings and is often confused with the more illustrious, but unrelated, de la Pole family. The Poles had a tenuous link to the Tudors through Geoffrey Pole, a Buckinghamshire squire whose wife, Edith, was the half-sister of Margaret Beaufort, Henry VII's mother.

Following Richard III's death at Bosworth, Henry Tudor brokered the marriage between Edith's son Richard and Lady Margaret, daughter of the Duke of Clarence, niece of two Yorkist kings: Edward IV and Richard III, and the granddaughter of Richard Neville, the Earl of Warwick. The mingling of Margaret's Plantagenet and Yorkist blood cast a shadow over her family as rivals to Henry Tudor's claim to the throne, and the marriage was necessary as a show of loyalty to the Tudors.

Unfortunately, her younger brother Edward became a focus for those seeking an alternative claim as he was the only legitimate male Plantagenet heir to the throne. The new Tudor king was already grappling with insurrection and attempted invasions, and Edward was executed in 1499, just prior to Katherine of Aragon's arrival in England, in what was deemed a necessary act to secure the Tudor throne. Margaret wisely remained silent.

Richard Pole first served as Lord Chamberlain for Prince Arthur, and Margaret served as lady-in-waiting to the young princess, Katherine, as trusted members of the court and the fortunes of their four sons, Henry, Arthur, Reginald and Geoffrey, and daughter, Ursula, showed every promise. With Arthur's death in 1502, Katherine's household was dissolved, and Margaret lost her position. Her fortunes waned further when her husband died just three years later, leaving her with five children and very little else. On the brink of ruin, Margaret took lodgings at Syon Abbey, possibly with her two youngest children. Her eldest son, Henry, was made a royal ward, while Reginald was destined for a life in the Church.

But these noble families were never entirely without resources, and with the ascension of Henry VIII, the Poles enjoyed a swift return to wealth and prestige. Margaret returned to serve Queen Katherine of Aragon and Henry VIII granted her a hereditary title, Countess of Salisbury, which made Margaret one of the wealthiest peers in the country. Her eldest son, Henry, was created Baron Montagu and Arthur would serve as one of six Gentlemen of the Privy Chamber, until his death in 1526.

Henry VIII was especially fond of Reginald and, after the latter graduated from Oxford University, Henry heaped ecclesiastical rewards on him, despite the fact that Reginald was not yet ordained as a priest. Henry went on to fund his cousin's matriculation at the University of Padua, a beneficence he would later come to regret.

After 20 years of marriage, Henry's determination to divorce Katherine had far-reaching effects. The loyalties of many noble families, particularly the Poles, lay with Katherine. Henry must have recognized that his relationship with Anne Boleyn was unpopular and so he tried to bribe

Reginald to gain his support, offering him the lucrative Archbishopric of York and the Diocese of Winchester. But Pole rebuffed him and returned to Europe, dividing his time between Italy and France. In *The Mirror and the Light*, Cromwell gives a rather acerbic appraisal of Reginald: 'The plain exterior gives no idea of the elaborate, useless nature of his mind, with its little shelves and niches for scruples and doubts.' Reginald had many grave doubts about his royal cousin, from his divorce to his title of Supreme Head of the Church. He was under the illusion that he could publicly criticize and attack Henry while remaining out of reach – but his family were not.

THE COURTENAYS

While the family could trace their roots to France, unlike so many others, the Courtenays did not come to England following the Norman invasion; their story is rather less glorious. In the 12th century, Reginald de Courtenay quarrelled with the French king, Louis VII, and was forced to flee to England. He left behind several members of his family, including his daughter, who was promptly married, along with her family titles, to the king's younger brother, Peter, who became Peter I of Courtenay. The family was now divided in two, with both branches connected to their respective crowns. Successive generations of Courtenays built on the family foundations, earning titles, wealth and status for their military prowess. They became an integral part of the royal fabric, with Sir Hugh Courtenay esteemed as one of the founding members of the Most Noble Order of the Garter, firmly establishing the family as part of England's noble elite.

By the 15th century, there were two main branches of Courtenays derived from the two sons of Hugh Courtenay, Earl of Devon, the eldest – and heir – Hugh Courtenay, and his younger brother, Philip. The latter formed what was known as a cadet line, and Cromwell would work well with William Courtenay, one of his descendants. With marriage still the best route to power, a marriage was arranged between William's widowed daughter-in-law Catherine St Leger, a cousin of Anne Boleyn, and Cromwell's nephew, Richard, which Anne objected to. Cromwell's relationship with the main branch of Courtenays, however, could not have been more different.

This line, descended from Hugh Courtenay, was considered one of the most noble and influential families in the country and, like the Poles, they could point to a very special royal lineage when, early on, William Courtenay married Catherine of York, the daughter of King Edward IV and Elizabeth Woodville. His son, Henry Courtenay, was a close childhood friend and cousin of the future Henry VIII, who appointed him as a Gentleman of the

Privy Chamber, and he also held a position on the Privy Council. Henry was an ideal companion for the young King Henry – both were athletic and physically fit. The two young men were inseparable, and Henry indulged his cousin with the traditional hereditary titles and positions which had previously belonged to the family, such as High Steward of the Duchy of Cornwall. But the pinnacle of Courtenay's career came with his elevation as Earl of Devon, and Marquess of Exeter, re-establishing the titles of his forebears.

Courtenay was highly influential at court, and though the family publicly supported the regime – even when it came to the dangerous matters of the Oath of Succession and the Act of Supremacy – they despised Thomas Cromwell, and he them. Courtenay and his wife, Gertrude, were close to Katherine of Aragon, taking her side in the divorce matter. They made clear their distaste for Anne by refusing to attend her coronation. Henry was furious and demanded proof of loyalty by choosing Gertrude as godmother to Anne's daughter, Princess Elizabeth. But it was a poor choice.

Privately the Courtenays regarded Mary as the true heir to the throne, and Gertrude became one of Chapuy's most trusted informants. They came dangerously close to committing treason when, like other conservatives of court, they met with Elizabeth Barton, the Holy Maid of Kent (see Chapter 3). Following her arrest, they quickly sought to distance themselves, though others who had visited her, notably Bishop John Fisher, were arrested.

Gertrude Courtenay was pardoned and begged Cromwell to protect her and her husband from further censure. Mantel's Cromwell advises her what to write in a letter to Henry; he recommends that she grovel, but Gertrude's real letter to Henry was contrite and well-crafted as she took the blame upon herself. From 1533 onwards, Cromwell's relationship with conservative factions such as the Courtenays and the Poles improved as his own relationship with Anne deteriorated and they played a small part in the machinations which contributed to her fall. It was an alliance borne of necessity, but one from which Cromwell was quick to extricate himself once Jane Seymour became queen. The two sides soon reverted to mutual suspicion and hostility, with Mantel's Cromwell sending Thomas Wyatt's mistress, Bess Darrell, into both the Pole and Courtenay households to glean any talk of treason. For now, Cromwell remained master of everything.

SUCCESS AND SUCCESSION

The year 1536 had been an extraordinary one. The country witnessed the death of one queen, the execution of another and the creation of a third – and all by the end of May. In *The Mirror and the Light* it is Thomas Boleyn who profoundly encapsulates what everyone must have felt: 'We have seen such times, Lord Cromwell, events crowded into a week, that in ordinary times would have sustained the chroniclers for a decade.' Cromwell now had an unprecedented, overarching view of the entire governmental system. His offices included: Lord Privy Seal, Master of the King's Jewels, Keeper of the Hanaper, Chancellor of the Exchequer, and Principal Secretary. Henry also allowed him to retain his religious title of Vicegerent or Vicar General, granted the previous year, thus an enormous degree of political power was now in the hands of a single minister of the king, rather than several. As Jane Seymour notes: 'It is a thing never seen before, Lord Cromwell is the government, and the church as well.'

Socially, Cromwell was equally in demand – he hunted, hawked, gambled and enjoyed dice in particular, he put on elaborate entertainments for the king at his own expense, his kitchens received game from Lubeckian merchants and ambassadors. He also spent a small fortune on wine. He continued to work well with those he had placed close to the throne, namely the Seymours, and the new queen and her family knew to whom they owed their success and their ever-rising fortunes. Cromwell and the court hoped the novelty of this peaceful new life would last, and that Henry would be less fractious, less unpredictable. But Henry was no longer the fit, athletic man of his youth; his leg had never healed following the jousting accident in January, and, through Cromwell's eyes, we see the more mercurial Henry emerging – autocratic and increasingly difficult to predict.

Mantel's Cromwell keeps a journal, *The Book Called Henry*, in which he writes advice for his protégés on how to deal with the king, but as time goes by, he finds he has less and less to write, and what he has written is of no use in managing an increasingly dangerous monarch. Jane, on the other hand, begins to prove herself far more adept at managing Henry, though she struggles to convince him to allow his daughter Mary back into the fold. In this matter, both she and Mary underestimated Henry's absolute determination to force Mary to submit, as her mother never had. Mary believed that with Anne's death, Henry would welcome her back at court, but this notion was quickly dashed by Henry's vehement insistence that Mary recognize that her mother's marriage had been invalid, and that therefore that she is illegitimate. The second Act of Succession of 1536, declared both Henry's daughters bastards, thereby removing them from the line of succession – and that, if he had no legitimate male children, Henry could nominate his heir.

Heirs become a frequent theme in *The Mirror and the Light*, as Henry thunders into middle age, increasingly unwell, with aches and pains, petulant and bad-tempered, 'dragging his new weight'. We are drawn into the personal lives of the young contenders around Henry: Henry's illegitimate son, Henry Fitzroy and his young wife, Mary Fitzroy, daughter of the Duke of Norfolk; the king's niece, Margaret Douglas; and his eldest daughter, Lady Mary. In *The Mirror and the Light*, their various intrigues are laid across Cromwell's desk roughly at the same time, dramas so entwined that it is difficult to pick everything apart.

THE LADY MARY

The Lady Mary is Cromwell's chief concern, and he has been grappling with her rehabilitation since 1535. In *Bring Up the Bodies*, she is uppermost in his mind as Henry lies unconscious following his jousting accident, much to Anne's displeasure. But as Cromwell argues reasonably with Anne, he cannot hold a country with her baby in the cradle, therefore the young Mary is his first choice. Mary and her relationship with her father and with Cromwell form a large part of *The Mirror and the Light*, a reflection of her growing importance following Anne's death after years of neglect and exile.

Without her mother to continue her fight against Henry, Mary grew into a role of a beloved daughter, revered throughout the country and valued by her father. By 1536 the line of succession had become tangled: an illegitimate son, two illegitimate daughters, a nephew and a niece. Cromwell believed that if Henry were to die only Mary could unite the country. We know that within weeks of Anne's execution the real Mary wrote to Cromwell begging him to intercede with her father on her behalf, but in *The Mirror and the Light*, Cromwell tells Chapuys that Mary must recognize that her mother's marriage was unlawful and that she is not the king's heir. Cromwell warns Chapuys to advise her to capitulate: 'If Mary enrages her father, it will come to your door,' a warning heeded by Chapuys. Mantel draws on history to show how closely Chapuys and Cromwell worked together to restore Mary.

Cromwell's early letters to Mary, supported by Chapuys, showed a genuine concern for her. Since Elizabeth's birth, Mary had lived at Hatfield, forced to serve in her half-sister's household. Anne's paternal aunts, Lady Anne Shelton and her sister Alice Boleyn, managed the household from 1533 onwards, and during this time tried to persuade Mary to accept the title of 'Lady' as opposed to 'Princess'. Lady Shelton was repeatedly chastised by Anne Boleyn for showing too much sympathy for the young girl. In *The Mirror and the Light*, Cromwell enjoys a close relationship with Lady Shelton and her husband, noting that she harbours no ill will towards him for the execution of her niece. Cromwell also sends Rafe Sadler and Thomas Wriothesley to visit Mary and explain her position, their respectful tones contrasting with the aggressive approach of the Duke of Norfolk and Bishop Sampson, who were sent by Henry on the same errand.

In the midst of this battle of wills between Mary and her father, Reginald Pole sent his royal cousin a copy of his treatise, *Pro ecclesiasticae unitatis defensione*, a strong denunciation of Henry's position as head of the English church; it also attacked Henry's claim of royal supremacy and his second marriage. Reginald also called on the princes of Europe to depose Henry, without recognizing that such an act of treason endangered not only his family, but also Mary, whom he sought to champion.

As Mantel's Henry rages: 'You see how it all works together? Pole exhorts Europe to take arms against me, and at the very same hour, my own daughter defies me.' But rumours spread that the Poles and Courtenays planned to marry Reginald Pole to Mary Tudor and overthrow the king. To make matters much worse, Mary received numerous messages from the Pole family, and Gertrude Courtenay even visited her. Henry dismissed Henry Courtenay from the Privy Council and would become fixated on finding Reginald, and either having him brought to England to face justice or, even better, assassinated.

Cromwell and Chapuys became greatly alarmed as Henry prepared legal proceedings against Mary, which could result in her execution, a move that shocked his own Privy Council. When William FitzWilliam, Henry's

Treasurer, spoke out against the proposal, he was summarily dismissed from the Council. The scene appears in *The Mirror and the Light*, with Cromwell pulling off FitzWilliam's chain of office as he pushes him out of the room. But Henry assumes, rightly, it is only for show as he knows Cromwell is in agreement. Mantel's Cromwell works with Chapuys to resolve Mary's situation, then feigns despair at failing the king, and pretends that he fears for his reputation, even his life. But historically his fear was genuine. Henry ordered the arrests of several men who had been allies of Cromwell and acted against anyone who supported Mary. Several of Cromwell's friends and supporters were brought in for questioning, thus Cromwell had every reason to feel anxious.

In *The Mirror and the Light*, Cromwell summons Francis Bryan to the Tower for an interview. Cromwell knows that Francis, together with his brother-in-law, Nicholas Carew, supported Mary's restoration as rightful heir, as did the Poles and Courtenays. Bryan's mother, Lady Margaret, had been Mary and Elizabeth's governess, and Cromwell instructs Bryan to visit his mother and ask her to persuade Mary to submit to her father. For now all efforts must be made to save Mary from her father, and herself.

This was a critical moment for Henry and for Mary, and Mantel frames the collaboration of Cromwell and Chapuys to resolve the situation from historical records. It is more than likely that they would have met to discuss what Mary should write to her father. Although Mantel places Cromwell with his son and nephew, sitting at his desk trying to choose just the words that will placate her father, we are not entirely sure who drafted Mary's letter. In his despatch to Charles V, Chapuys wrote that he had 'put down in writing several candid and temperate statements'. Mantel gives these statements to Cromwell, though we may allow that Chapuys had decided to omit Cromwell's involvement to his master.

Throughout *The Mirror and the Light*, Cromwell's relationship with Mary is ambiguous but there are seemingly elements of passion, the meaning of which remain just out of reach to the reader. In *The Mirror and the Light*, Mary's scenes with Cromwell convey her pain and turmoil at betraying one parent for the love of the other. It is Rafe Sadler who delivers the draft letter to Henry for Mary to sign, which she does without reading it. Mary wants it to be over: she wants to be restored to favour and unlike her mother, she takes no comfort in being a martyr. Finally, Mary is reunited in an emotional visit with her father and his new queen. From Jane she receives a large diamond ring, the weight and size of which is measured in a flash by Mantel's Henry as it is slipped onto Mary's tiny finger.

HENRY FITZROY

One person who was likely to have been keen for Mary to remain estranged from her father (and therefore out of the succession race) was Henry VIII's illegitimate son, Henry Fitzroy. Fitzroy, whose mother was one of Henry's most well-known mistresses, Elizabeth Blount, is a minor character in the first two books, and historically Fitzroy's value rose and fell depending on how many other legitimate heirs Henry was willing to acknowledge. Following Anne's death in 1536 we see a young man who for the first time feels that the throne is very much within his grasp.

It seems likely that Henry intended to make Fitzroy legitimate, making him Duke of Richmond and Somerset – even the name 'Fitzroy' comes from the Anglo-Norman, meaning 'son of the king'. The boy was raised like a prince, and, as for his half-sister Mary, Cardinal Wolsey was appointed as his godfather and was in charge of his upbringing. Mantel's Fitzroy maintains an affection for the long-dead Cardinal, which surprises Cromwell. As Fitzroy tells Cromwell, he barely saw his father as a child, but Wolsey gave him toys. There is evidence to support a close relationship between Wolsey and his godson, with the Cardinal sending young Fitzroy to Yorkshire to head up his own court and council.

Henry doted on his only son, immensely proud of siring such a healthy and athletic boy, proof that his lack of legitimate male heirs was not his doing. We do not know what Fitzroy felt for his father, but Mantel's version has no love for him, and becomes fixated on the crown. Cromwell suspects this is Fitzroy's father-in-law, the Duke of Norfolk's doing, or that of his brother-in-law, Henry Howard. Certainly the marriage between Fitzroy and Mary Howard in 1533 was most advantageous for the Howards, but would give Norfolk a dangerous amount of power should Fitzroy become king.

Despite Fitzroy's position, and his belief that he was the logical choice, Chapuys believed he would not be considered, as by mid-1536 the young man was very ill, likely from consumption or lung disease. Mantel's Cromwell also firmly tries to disabuse Fitzroy of the notion that he might be king, or that he, Cromwell, has the power to persuade Henry. Mantel's Cromwell makes the salient point that while Fitzroy may be a boy, he is still the son of a mistress – Mary and Elizabeth are at least daughters of queens.

Margaret Douglas

Margaret Douglas was the daughter of Henry's sister Margaret and her second husband, Archibald Douglas. They had married during her regency for her two-year-old heir, James V. The marriage caused a civil war in Scotland as warring factions tried to take the crown. Margaret was forced to flee across the border with her daughter to England, with young Margaret being sent to stay in Cardinal Wolsey's household. Following the Cardinal's death, Margaret was first transferred to the household of her cousin Princess Mary, where the two formed a close connection, before finally joining Anne Boleyn's retinue. Diarmaid MacCulloch describes Margaret as a 'loose cannon in the realm' and indeed, while serving Anne, Margaret formed a secret attachment to Thomas Howard, the younger half-brother of the Duke of Norfolk.

In the series, the affair does not reach Cromwell's ears until after Anne's execution and he is frustrated that he has been so distracted by the chaos that he missed a dangerous relationship between a Howard and a potential heir to the throne. Historically, the affair was a small though troubling event in Henry's reign, but its literary impact was far more significant.

Mantel's Cromwell comes into the possession of a volume that contains almost 200 anonymous poems. This manuscript is one of the most important collections of Tudor courtly verse, written predominantly by the young women who served Anne Boleyn – Margaret Douglas, Mary Fitzroy, and Mary (or Margaret) Shelton, with some additions by Thomas and Henry Howard and Thomas Wyatt. The folio, known as *The Devonshire Manuscript*, housed in the British Library, provides a revealing insight into how men and women expressed themselves while negotiating courtly love, power, faith and politics; it is one of the most valuable surviving records of early Tudor poetry and the literary lives of Tudor women. But to Mantel's Cromwell and Wriothesley, it provides evidence of an illicit affair that could have had serious dynastic ramifications.

Mantel's Cromwell and Wriothesley interview Margaret Douglas, who is supported by her closest friend Mary Fitzroy. They quickly discover that the affair had gone well beyond courtly love, with Margaret insisting that they have been betrothed before witnesses. Mantel's Cromwell quietly urges Margaret to deny the betrothal but she names other women

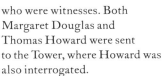

who were witnesses. Both Margaret Douglas and Thomas Howard were sent to the Tower, where Howard was also interrogated.

Cromwell casts his net to bring in the young women who once served Anne Boleyn and who knew about Margaret Douglas and Thomas Howard, including Mary Shelton, Anne's cousin, and Jane Rochford, George Boleyn's widow (see chapter 4). An enraged Henry has Cromwell draw up the Bill of Attainder which would allow the crown to convict Howard without a trial, on the grounds that the relationship is a threat to the peace and unity of the realm and so constituted high treason. The bill also forbade any marriage to a female member of the royal family without the king's assent. As Cromwell says: 'The new clauses won't necessarily stop royal persons doing stupid things. But they will create a formal process for dealing with them, when they do.' On 18 July 1536, Howard was attainted and awaited a traitor's death, though no execution was planned. Henry, still furious at his niece, kept her in the Tower, but allowed her to move to Syon Abbey when she fell ill, where she remained under house arrest.

Five days after the young Thomas Howard was attainted, Henry Fitzroy died at St James's Palace. There was no state funeral; instead it was left to the Duke of Norfolk to make the arrangements for his son-in-law. Norfolk planned to have him interred at Thetford Priory, the ancestral resting place of the Howard family. It should have been fairly simple to transport the body from London to Norfolk in a dignified manner but somehow the decaying body ended up in a straw-filled wagon, followed by only two mourners. Henry was understandably incandescent with rage at such negligence. Norfolk wrote to Cromwell, mortified that his plans for the internment should have gone so awry. At the time of the letter, Norfolk was hosting Cromwell's son Gregory, as part of a plan to immerse Gregory in high society. It marked the end of an era that proud Norfolk would be honoured to host the son of a man he had for years dismissed and disparaged.

RELIGION, THE DISSOLUTION OF THE MONASTERIES AND THE PILGRIMAGE OF GRACE

Throughout the medieval period, the Catholic Church was the spiritual authority and the lives of the people revolved around it. Everyone attended mass faithfully, sought forgiveness when necessary, and prayed for the dead to hasten their time in purgatory. Each day was punctuated by prayers which marked the passage of the hours and those who were literate read from the Book of Hours, a collection of biblical texts and prayers and elements of the liturgy. The most important book was the Bible, the text of which was in Latin, the language of the church. It was the role of the clergy to act as intermediaries and to interpret God's word for the masses, a position that gave great power to its priests and nuns.

Throughout Europe, there was no other religious alternative and any discontent with the authority of the church or attempt to reform its practices was silenced. The Church was immensely powerful with an established hierarchy. This hierarchy provided not only spiritual guidance, but became a political and financial empire with its own army; it negotiated peace and war, and bargained with the princes of Europe. Favours could be bought, wealth could be made, and corruption was rife.

The seeds of discontent with the church had been festering across Europe since the Middle Ages. In the late 14th century, Oxford scholar and church dissident John Wycliffe protested against indulgences and other practices which he regarded as the corruption of the Church. He argued that a layperson should be able to read God's words in a bible of their own language and oversaw an English translation. In Wittenberg, Germany, Martin Luther, a professor of theology, composer, priest and monk, rejected several teachings and practices of the Church, particularly the sale of indulgences, and his *Ninety-five Theses* made Luther a prominent figure in the Protestant Reformation.

Throughout Mantel's series, we catch glimpses of the men who steered the Reformation – John Calvin, Desiderius Erasmus, Huldrych Zwingli, Martin Bucer, Wycliffe and Luther. Cromwell read and owned their books – regarded as heretical by the church – but it is difficult to pinpoint his faith. Mantel's Cromwell states simply: 'I believe, but I do not believe enough'. Mantel is careful that her Cromwell does not identify with any particular religious philosophy, or in her words, 'explain himself', but two of the

greatest influences on Cromwell's spirituality were Erasmus and William Tyndale. Luther became a particular cause of Henry's, for different reasons.

Martin Luther

Luther was born in 1483 in Eisleben, Saxony, and by 1507 had been ordained as a priest, but over the next ten years he rejected many of the church's teachings. His key doctrine was that salvation or redemption was attainable only through faith in Christ, that is justification by faith alone. Aided by the Gutenberg printing press and woodcuts by Lucas Cranach, the controversies of matters such as church indulgences were made a matter for the general public. Pamphlets were widely dispersed in Germany one day and read in Paris the next.

A deeply conventional Catholic, in 1521 Henry took it upon himself to repudiate Luther in writing, accusing him of being 'a venomous serpent, a pernicious plague, infernal wolf, an infectious soul, a detestable trumpeter of pride, calumnies and schism'. But a spiritual debate had been ignited in Europe to determine, among other issues, how people reached salvation, how and by whom the Bible should be interpreted, the presence of Christ in the sacrament of Holy Communion, and the Holy Trinity.

Desiderius Erasmus

Erasmus, a leading philosopher and humanist thinker, was invited to England in 1499, to meet the boy who he hoped would be England's Renaissance prince.

Erasmus was sceptical of Luther's assertions, and is described by many as a Christian humanist, with a philosophy of life that combined Christian thought with classical traditions. Neither Erasmus nor Luther wanted their works associated with the other – although Erasmus had been an early critic of the Church and it is believed that the reformation could not have happened without him. When he was accused of laying the egg that Luther hatched, he responded that he laid a hen's egg, and Luther had hatched a chick of a very different feather. Erasmus was lauded for his Latin and Greek versions of the New Testament, which would become important texts throughout the Reformation and the Counter Reformation.

Cromwell may not have been a patron and friend of Erasmus like Thomas More or Thomas Boleyn, but we do know he held the scholar in high esteem.

When Mantel's Cromwell finds himself in the tower in 1540, it is Erasmus' book, *De praeparatione ad mortem*, that he reads, the very work Thomas Boleyn had commissioned from Erasmus seven years previously.

WILLIAM TYNDALE

Cromwell was also connected to William Tyndale, an English scholar and priest, who had also been influenced by Erasmus' Greek edition of the New Testament, but when he petitioned to be allowed to translate the Bible into English, he was censured and he left England for Germany. The first printing of William Tyndale's English New Testament was completed in 1526 in Worms, Germany, while smaller editions were smuggled into England; in *Wolf Hall*, Liz Cromwell receives the secret package along with Cromwell's longed-for Castilian soap. It was condemned by Henry, Wolsey and More. However, Henry would come to agree with Tyndale on some key issues, not because of any new-found faith, but rather because such arguments suited him, namely Tyndale's *Obedience of a Christian Man*, which argued that authority belonged to kings in their own realm, rather than the Pope. Unfortunately for Henry, Tyndale also believed that his first marriage was valid and criticized his pursuit of an annulment.

Historically, Cromwell was at the forefront of attempts to entice Tyndale back to England to write in defence of Henry's annulment, with his friend, Stephen Vaughan meeting with Tyndale in person, but to no avail. Tyndale's works made him a wanted man throughout Europe and he was always one step ahead of the authorities. He was eventually betrayed, arrested and taken to the castle of Vilvoorde, the great state prison of the Low Countries, and charged with heresy.

THE DISSOLUTION OF THE MONASTERIES

Before his fall and death in 1530, Cardinal Wolsey had already begun a series of reforms of monasteries, much of which was carried out by his assistant, Cromwell. They had the authority of Parliament to suppress houses with fewer than 12 monks and transfer their assets to royal colleges at Windsor and Cambridge, and to unite others with larger institutions; no houses were suppressed 'where God was well served', only those 'where most vice, mischief and abomination of living was used'. But when Henry failed to receive a satisfactory answer from Pope Clement in regards to the dissolution of his marriage to

Katherine, he declared himself Supreme Head of the Church of England, and used his newly created Reformation Parliament to pass a series of laws that fundamentally changed the nature of Parliament and the English government. In 1534, Cromwell was appointed to undertake an inventory of the income of every ecclesiastical estate of England and Wales, including the monasteries, to assess their value. After all, these properties now belonged to the English crown, not to Rome. Henry had ushered in the English Reformation and every monastery must submit to the king's authority.

THE PILGRIMAGE OF GRACE

The pace of religious change in the early years of the Reformation was too great for many in various areas of the country and not everyone was ready to embrace the break with Rome. Civic unrest morphed into civic insurrection. The autumn of 1536 saw violent religious riots against the king's Dissolution of the Monasteries in York and Lincolnshire. Previous rebellions had come to nothing, but this one would quickly become an uprising that almost brought the Tudor dynasty to its knees.

The people of the North had long felt neglected and overlooked by a king who had never once visited its counties. Religious change, coupled with a bad harvest and the ever-impending threat of higher taxes, enraged the common people, who blamed Cromwell for leading the country to ruin. Henry ordered the dukes of Norfolk and Suffolk and George Talbot, the Earl of Shrewsbury, to muster their loyal troops to suppress any possible insurrection. Cromwell wrote a letter to Thomas Boleyn, well respected and honoured in his county of Kent, to muster troops, which he did despite the letter being delayed by almost a week, giving him three days to comply. It speaks volumes that Thomas managed to gather 300 men and march to London.

Suffolk managed to contain the situation in Lincolnshire but in Yorkshire the rebels had rallied around a charismatic leader named Robert Aske, a well-connected lawyer who, like Cromwell, was a member of Gray's Inn. Aske was able to marshal a rabble into a single united force which swelled as it moved south to York and Pontefract. He was careful in presenting the rebellion as a sacred mission and crafted their demands: Henry was to halt his suppression of the monasteries and restore what had been destroyed; Mary was to be reinstated as heir (without any male progeny Henry had no legal succession – he had disinherited them all); the architects of Henry's religious programme, namely Cromwell and Audley, were to be executed, or at the very least exiled; and Cranmer and the other evangelical bishops were to be burned as heretics.

In *The Mirror and the Light*, Jane Seymour, who is often coached by Cromwell and her brothers, startles everyone by publicly beseeching her husband to allow his people to return to the old ways. We know that on numerous occasions Jane did plead the case for the rebels. Henry did not tolerate her interference and she was angrily rebuffed and warned not to meddle in royal affairs; however, in Mantel's version, Henry indicates that he will listen to her complaints when she bears him a son.

Henry was conciliatory toward Aske, and invited him to Greenwich for Christmas, promising safe conduct. Henry used Jane as a beacon for the rebels, who approved of her conservative piety, and promised that she would be crowned in York. Aske left court satisfied, with a message of peace and a promise from Henry that he would open a parliament in the North to decide any further religious matters. However, within weeks a small revolt sprang up, and although it had nothing to do with Aske, it gave Henry a much-needed excuse to renege on his promises and arrest Aske together with dozens of rebels. In May 1537, eleven people, including Aske, were tried and later executed.

Cromwell had taken the rebellion seriously and understood the ramifications had fortunes been different. Now more than ever he was determined to press on with religious change.

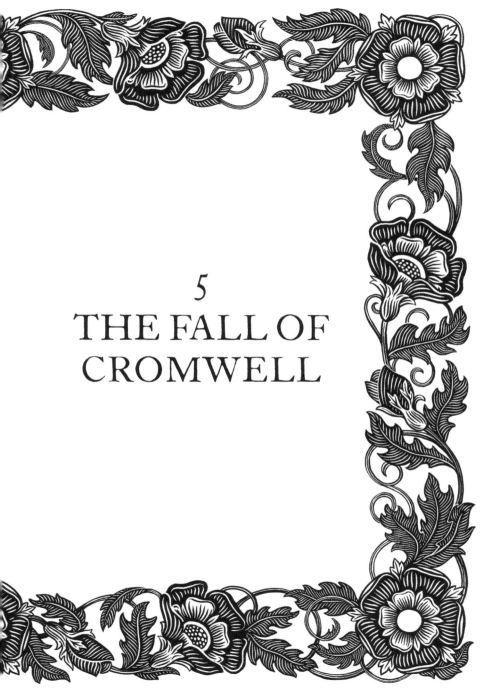

5

THE FALL OF CROMWELL

The king's vicious handling of the Pilgrimage of Grace and its leaders did not sit well with the people, who recalled their king being more benevolent in his youth. Cromwell remained deeply unpopular outside London but his countless duties kept him occupied. Mantel's Cromwell hears of the rebels' last days before they are executed, cursing Thomas Cromwell's name. He warns Mary not to speak in their defence, and notes that Jane has likely been warned by her brother.

Peace became the theme of the new year. The rebellions had encouraged further religious reform, and in February 1537, Cromwell convened a vicegerential synod – a council of the church. His opening speech called for a calm debate of theological issues, a timely plea considering the very first item on the agenda concerned the sacrament, a sore point between Catholics and reformers. All religious changes bore the stamp of Cromwell and his colleagues, Cranmer and Edward Fox, and Henry seemed to approve of his Privy Seal's reforms, but Cromwell's political authority had taken a blow following the Pilgrimage of Grace and he faced stern opposition from the Duke of Norfolk.

Cromwell was also active as the chief architect of diplomacy, much to Norfolk's annoyance, who always preferred a French alliance to an Imperial alliance. In March 1537 we know that Thomas Wyatt, who had returned to some degree of favour, was sent as ambassador to the court of Charles V, ostensibly to improve relations and negotiate a marriage arrangement between Mary and Charles' son, but also to prevent Charles from moving closer to France – the usual game of diplomacy. Cromwell may have been fond of Wyatt and had saved his life more than once, but he grew frustrated with Wyatt's carelessness, and penchant for spending more than he earned, something we see in *The Mirror and the Light*.

After the death and destruction of 1536, marriages, coronations and births must have been welcome themes in 1537. Chapuys reported that Jane's coronation was due to take place that summer, but speculated that Henry might hold off on such an expense until Jane proved she could carry an heir. Sometime in the spring of 1537 it was announced that Jane at last was pregnant, to the resounding joy of the country and to Henry's great relief. Ambassadors remarked that he was more attentive than he had ever been, if that were possible, and when she developed cravings for quails he made sure plenty were shipped across from Calais.

Gregory Cromwell was also now of a marriageable age, and Cromwell had his sights set on Bess Seymour, Jane's younger sister. Historically, Bess wrote to Cromwell in March of 1537 to ask for financial assistance. Their relationship appears to have been quite close, and Mantel places them in conversation in 1537. In a humorous example of crossed wires, Bess believes Cromwell intends to marry her himself, which would certainly solve her financial difficulties.

Bess and Gregory were married sometime in the summer of 1537. The match was ambitious and placed Cromwell in an interesting position – his son was now brother-in-law to the king, and what did that make him? In *The Mirror and the Light*, it is the increasingly inscrutable Wriothesley who casually remarks that who would have thought Gregory would be so useful in uniting Cromwell with the king's family. One wonders if Cromwell felt uneasy at how dangerous this might be.

A BIRTH AND A DEATH

Jane's pregnancy had progressed well, and on 9 October she went into labour, a long and agonizing ordeal that lasted for two days. Finally, on the 11 October, the bells rang out that Henry and Jane had been delivered of a prince. Jane had triumphed.

The child, Edward, was robust and healthy, and on 15 October the infant was christened in an opulent ceremony in the chapel royal at Hampton Court. As was the custom, the king rewarded his favourites with titles and land – Edward Seymour was made Earl of Hertford and Thomas Seymour was elevated to the Privy Chamber. William FitzWilliam was also rewarded with the Earldom of Southampton, but Cromwell received nothing. Mantel's Cromwell worries that his failure to capture Reginald Pole has displeased Henry enough to withhold an elevation, although in August he had been inducted into the prestigious Order of the Garter.

However, the celebrations were short-lived. The day after the christening Jane complained of nausea and fever; within a few days she began to weaken and on 24 October she died. Henry was inconsolable and the whole nation went into mourning. In *The Mirror and the Light*, Jane's sister, Bess, tells Cromwell that Jane was lucky and unlucky: lucky to become queen of England, and unlucky to die of it. Jane was buried in St George's Chapel at Windsor, and she was given a moving epitaph:

Here lies Jane, a phoenix who died in giving another phoenix birth. Let her be mourned, for birds like these are rare indeed.

THE SEARCH FOR A NEW QUEEN

This was the first time Henry had been left without a wife, and for the first time he did not have a successor waiting in the wings. Cromwell and Henry's councillors were divided as to whether they should look to France or the Holy Roman Empire for a suitable candidate. Henry was roused from his mourning stupor by the prospect of a pretty bride as the line-up began. In *The Mirror and the Light* Cromwell lists a number of royal and noble women who might be suitable, but Henry already has his own favourite, namely Mary de Guise, and is piqued when Cromwell informs him that it appears she is to marry James V of Scotland.

Undeterred, Henry proposed the match to the French ambassador Louis de Perreau, Sieur de Castillon. In the historical meeting, which began neutrally and quickly went downhill, Castillon suggested other options. Henry demanded that he must see the woman in person before making a decision, to which the real Castillon is said to have said curtly that it was not custom to send ladies to another court as if they were horses to be bought. Would Henry insist on mounting them too before making his choice? The real Castillon wrote that Henry was immediately embarrassed and tried to make light of the conversation, but Mantel's Castillon goes further: 'Has your Majesty considered that it might be difficult to find any lady to marry you at all?' 'Why?' the king asks. 'Because you kill your wives.' While there is no evidence that Castillon went so far, he did leave England very soon after the meeting, to be replaced by Charles de Marillac.

Cromwell continued to press for an Imperial match, and historically Henry was interested in Christina of Milan, the niece of Charles V: 16 years old, pretty and the daughter of the former King of Denmark. Henry begged the Emperor, via Chapuys, to arrange a set of marriages: Mary to Charles's nephew, Dom Luis of Portugal, and Henry himself to Christina. Hans Holbein was sent to paint Christina's portrait, which Henry became entranced by. But then Henry requested that Christina come to Calais, accompanied by her aunt, Mary of Hungary, so that he could meet her, a ludicrous notion which made Chapuys cringe even as he wrote the dispatch.

Cromwell was well aware that while Henry tarried, his two rivals, Charles and Francis, were on the brink of securing what looked like a lasting peace agreement, leaving the excommunicated Henry out in the cold. We know that Cromwell urged Wyatt to remain involved in the negotiations to ensure England played some small part, but when the news of the agreement broke in England, it was clear that the truce of Aigues-Mortes had no role for

Henry. Crucially, it also emerged that Henry's cousin, Reginald Pole, had been involved in the negotiations, which Henry believed was evidence that an invasion of England, with a potential new king at the helm, was imminent.

Amidst the marriage game, in May 1538, Henry fell dangerously ill. It is believed that a blood clot had lodged in his lung, and for almost two weeks it was unclear whether Henry would recover. Mantel's Cromwell asks himself who he should ride to or from, should Henry die.

CROMWELL STRIKES

Cromwell was determined to stamp out any rival claims to the throne and the Poles were at the top of his list. In August of 1538 Cromwell made his move knowing that Geoffrey was in contact with his older brother, Reginald.

Geoffrey was kept in a damp cell in the Tower for two months in order to break him, and it worked. Geoffrey revealed the family's secrets, implicating his older brothers as well as Henry Courtenay, one of Henry's oldest friends. On 4 November Henry Courtenay and Hugh Pole were beheaded on Tower Hill alongside accused co-conspirator Sir Edward Neville. Geoffrey was eventually released, but there is evidence to suggest that he was never the same again.

In the New Year, another conspirator was sent to the Tower, but one which surprised those at court – Sir Nicholas Carew, Master of the Horse, and another of Henry's close friends. The reasons for his imprisonment were not exactly clear – although he had always maintained links with the Pole family and corresponded with both, this was not a secret. He also sat on the jury which indicted Pole and Courtenay, and expressed scepticism of their guilt, which could have been a factor. Carew was executed in March 1539. Several months later, Cromwell brought a bill of attainder against Margaret Pole and Gertrude Courtenay, and both were sent to the Tower. Cromwell was clearing the chessboard.

NEW ALLIANCES AND
ANNE OF CLEVES

Cromwell's political vision for England in 1539 was unprecedented. He had tired of the same chessboard and the same pieces – Charles, Francis and Henry. When Anne Boleyn had been in power, he had entertained the notion of strengthening ties with reformers from German states and had been in secret communication with them through his agent, Thomas Tebold, the much doted on godson of Thomas Boleyn. He was particularly interested in the Schmalkaldic League, a military alliance founded by two of the most powerful protestant princes, Philip I and John Frederick of Saxony.

England began making overtures to the German states in 1531, but by 1539 Cromwell knew that an alliance with the German duchy of Cleves, a noble family whose lands in the north of Saxony bordered those of Charles V, could be of use. The Cleves family also enjoyed family ties to the Schmalkaldic League, which would also give Charles pause should he consider invading England. In *The Mirror and the Light* Cromwell and Wriothesley are already quietly discussing the possibility of Henry marrying one of the Duke of Cleves' daughters – Amalia or her sister, Anne.

Cromwell first became aware of Anne and her sister Amalia in a letter from one of his agents, John Hutton, in December of 1537, but only in 1539 did Cromwell seriously entertain the idea of one of them as a candidate as Henry's queen. Anne was born sometime in 1515, the second daughter of John III, Duke of Cleves and Maria, Duchess of Jülich-Berg. Henry had not been her first suitor – in 1511 she had been betrothed to the son and heir of the Duke of Lorraine, but the match had fallen through in 1535. As soon as Henry agreed to consider the alliance, Cromwell dispatched Holbein to the paint both Anne and Amalia.

During this period, Cromwell was plagued by ill health and suffered from an intermittent fever, which kept him away for court for days at a time. He also suffered from anxiety, believing his enemies whispered poison in the ear of the king, and perhaps he had cause, for Henry had a habit of believing the last person he spoke to. When Cromwell came back to court he found Stephen Gardiner had also returned after a three-year embassy to France, and was back in favour. Much as Wolsey once tried to have an audience with Henry in private, and found himself having to deliver his news in public, now the conservative Gardiner stood at Henry's side. While Cromwell had been away, the Duke of Norfolk had argued convincingly against Cromwell's proposed religious reforms. In 1539–40, Gardiner achieved a major victory over his reformist opponents: The act of the Six Articles was passed, confirming the supremacy of particular rights within the church of England, such as the role of the Eucharist and celibacy amongst the clergy. Cromwell had banked on royal support, but Henry, who had always been Catholic at heart, showed every intention of returning to the old ways.

But Cromwell was hopeful when Holbein's portraits of the Cleves sisters arrived in England and Henry fell for Anne's. Events still moved interminably slow for Cromwell, but Henry had accepted the match and the marriage treaty was agreed to in October 1539. Anne would not be like any of Henry's other wives: she had not received a formal education, she did not play an instrument, she did not hunt, nor did she speak any English. But these were minor issues Cromwell hoped to remedy. Mantel's Cromwell pitches the marriage to Henry: how grateful this young woman will be to be taken from such a life. Cromwell also hoped that the sweet, agreeable and meek young woman would remind him of Jane.

The court made ready for a new queen: members of the queen's household which had been disbanded following Jane's death now regrouped. Jane Rochford returned alongside the familiar names: Mary Fitzroy, Edward Seymour's wife, Anne, and Elizabeth (Bess) Cromwell. But there were a few new faces: Catherine Carey, the daughter of Mary Boleyn; Mary Norris, daughter of the deceased Henry Norris; and another Howard niece, Catherine. This is our first glimpse of Henry's fifth wife: 'Her glance slips absently over the men, but rakes the women head to toe. Clearly she has never seen so many great ladies before; she is studying how they stand, how they move.' Mantel's Cromwell expresses disappointment that Catherine, Lady Latimer, has not joined the household. He has been teased in the past by the boys at Austin Friars of setting his cap at her when she visited on behalf of her husband; he admits that he finds her to be highly intelligent and alluring. Cromwell, of course, does not know that Lady Latimer will, in time, be Henry's sixth wife.

Anne of Cleves' journey across the continent to England took a gruelling two weeks, taking her through Imperial territory for which she required a passport, and then through to Calais and across the Channel. It was intended that Anne should meet Henry for the first time at Blackheath, but an impetuous Henry could not contain himself and against everyone's advice, rode down to Rochester to surprise her, regardless of protocol or what her own entourage would make of it. In *The Mirror and the Light* it is Gregory Cromwell who barges into his father's room asking how he could let Henry go, as he recounts the mortifying incident.

Anne was watching the bull-baiting from her window when a commonly dressed Henry approached her. She barely acknowledged him, naturally, though some reports tell us that he tried to kiss her and she pushed him away. His romantic gesture rejected, Henry is crushed, embarrassed and ultimately repulsed. In his eyes, this tall, slim and pleasant young woman immediately becomes ugly, foul-smelling and certainly not the virgin he was promised. She has shown Henry his own reflection, and he hates her for it.

Henry believed he had been deceived, and demanded that the ambassadors accompanying Anne produce papers proving that she was free to marry. In the meantime, Henry reluctantly allowed the wedding to take place on 6 January 1540 in the Royal Chapel at Greenwich, but the couple's first night as husband and wife was far from rewarding. Henry was quick to tell Cromwell that he had not consummated the marriage, that he could not bring himself to do so. To make matters worse, word reached England that Charles V and Francis were withdrawing from their mutual alliance, and both now looked once more to England to renew their negotiations. But what really must have rankled with Henry was when he learned that Anne's brother, Wilhelm, might marry the woman he had desired, Christina, Duchess of Milan, as part of an agreement with Charles V.

MISCALCULATIONS AND EXECUTION

It is difficult for the reader to get a sense of Cromwell's downfall in *The Mirror and the Light* because he simply does not see it coming. The evidence, however, is manifestly clear as the conservative factions of the dukes of Norfolk and Suffolk, together with Stephen Gardiner, gathered against Cromwell, taking advantage of the king's displeasure with his most recent marriage.

In April 1540, Ambassador Marillac wrote to Francis I that Cromwell was finished, his downfall imminent. But Cromwell rallied, and met with his detractors in Parliament on 12 April and successfully passed a series of bills he had drafted in the hope that this would consolidate his position. He was particularly pleased with a new taxation bill which would increase crown revenue, which always pleased Henry. But then Cromwell miscalculated:

Before Norfolk arrives home from France, he has invaded the duke's own country. He has closed Thetford Priory, where the duke's forebears lie.

Closing Thetford Priory was an unforgivable insult to Norfolk. The duke asked that it at least be made into a college for the benefit of many. But an overly antagonistic Cromwell simply dissolved it, forcing the disinterment of the Howard tombs, which were moved to Framlingham.

Cromwell was feeling confident, believing that he had fought off a political attack. But within days he was surprised to hear that Wriothesley, whom he had considered his man for some years, was back in Gardiner's sphere. To borrow a phrase from the real Gardiner, 'the cat had been turned in the pan' meaning things were not as they should be. Cromwell, both historically and in the series, failed to understand Henry. He had tried to force his own religious ideas on the king, choosing to ignore the fact that Henry's break with Rome had been a political move to secure the annulment of his marriage, and while he relished his authority over the Church of England, he had no intention of ever committing to reformist doctrine. And Cromwell had, like Wolsey, made too many enemies.

However, if Cromwell had harboured any apprehension about his standing, his surprise elevation as Earl of Essex, on 18th April, one of the most ancient and distinguished titles in the country, as well as his appointment as Lord Great Chamberlain, was more than enough to help him feel secure. The timing of such prestigious titles still puzzles historians, with some speculating that Henry intended to lull Cromwell into a false sense of security. Cromwell was unaware of various accusations that were being voiced to the king: that he had intended to marry the Lady Mary; that he had negotiated with the princes of the Schmalkaldic League beyond his remit; that he had called into question Henry's virility over the non-consummation of his marriage to Anne of Cleves; and that Cromwell had been overheard saying he would fight for reform even if he had to take a sword in his hand. For an already paranoid, agitated and vengeful king, this was all the evidence he needed.

The meeting on 1 June 1540 should have been an ordinary gathering of the Privy Council. Cromwell arrived slightly late, surprised that his colleagues were about to start without him. As he sat, he was told the council did not sit with traitors. Mantel imagines the scene:

The councillors fall on him. They tug, kick, haul. He is barged and buffeted, his gold chain is off.

Marillac gleefully reports to Francis I how Cromwell was humiliated.

It was a blur. Cromwell was subject to a bill of attainder that denied him a trial. The charges cited grounds of treason and heresy – that he had been elevated from a base and low degree to a position of trust and power which he had abused, and was a heretic, but Henry needed Cromwell to attend to the arrangements that would extricate him from the Cleves marriage. Men who Cromwell previously trusted, like Wriothesley, Audley and Rich, proved to be, as Marillac wrote, men who bent to all winds. In *The Mirror and the Light*, he learns that Rich is pawing through Austin Friars to uncover further damning evidence.

The annulment of the Cleves marriage took only a few weeks, and when Anne was informed on 9 July, she was shocked but respectful of Henry's wishes, and took his rejection more gracefully than any other wife. Cromwell's imprisonment lasted seven weeks, during which Cromwell desperately wrote to Henry:

Sir, upon [my kne]es I most humbly beseech your most gracious Majesty [to be a goo]d and gracious lord to my poor son, the good and virtu[ous lady his] wife, and their poor children.

Mantel's Cromwell remembers the words of Erasmus: 'No man is to be despaired of, so long as the breath is in him.'

Cromwell signed his letter to the king: 'Written with the quaking hand and most sorrowful heart of your most sorrowful subject and most humble servant and prisoner.'

What Henry enjoyed more than anything, apart from a hunt, was a wedding and an execution, and if they were on the same day then so much the better. On 28 July, Cromwell walked the short distance from his cell in the Tower to the scaffold as Henry married the young Catherine Howard at Oatlands Palace in Surrey. The game of chess could begin again, with new players. In Cromwell's final minutes, his often-sung Italian folk song, 'Scaramella to the War is Gone', becomes muddled with one of Thomas Wyatt's poems: 'I am as I am and so will I be. But how that is I leave to you, false or true.' Words reminiscent of those spoken by Anne Boleyn: 'If anyone shall meddle with my cause I ask them to judge the best.' Anne's soul departed between sighs, Cromwell's between a pulse-beat.

'He is far from England now, far from these islands, from the waters salt and fresh. He has vanished. He feels for an opening, blinded, looking for a door: tracking the light along the wall.

THE AFTERMATH

We do not follow Cromwell in death, but many others would follow him to the scaffold: Margaret Pole, Jane Rochford, Catherine Howard, the Duke of Norfolk's son, Henry Howard, and both Seymour brothers, the men being executed on the orders of their nephew, Edward VI. Cromwell's boys – Rafe, Gregory and Richard – would struggle in the first year following Cromwell's death, but they all continued their careers at court, and remained close-knit throughout their lives. Gregory Cromwell would eventually participate in several high-profile parliamentary proceedings, including the attainders of Catherine Howard, and his father's enemies, Norfolk and his son, Henry Howard.

Although Cromwell's family publicly distanced themselves from the patriarch as Cromwell had likely recommended, he was mourned by them and loyal friends, and not least by the king. Marillac reported that Henry had raged at his councillors, 'saying that, upon light pretexts, by false accusations, they made him put to death the most faithful servant he ever had'. Henry never took accountability for his own poor decisions – it was always someone else's fault. Men like Rich, Wriothesley and Audley, who quietly side-stepped Cromwell's grisly fate, became Henry's new henchmen – Rich and Wriothesley's reputations forever tainted for racking the outspoken reformer Anne Askew with their own hands in 1546. Following Cromwell's death, Henry's court became more fractious and factional than it had ever been, with Henry becoming the irrational, tyrannical and vengeful monarch so well-known to history. Marillac, like Chapuys and other foreign ambassadors, had his measure, and he wrote frankly that Henry would go on dipping his hands in blood. It was more a prophesy than a speculation.

The real Cromwell once wrote to Thomas Wyatt that Henry was 'the Mirror and the light of all Kings and Princes in Christendom'. Henry was indeed the mirror, in whose reflection courtiers existed; and in whose light they thrived. But as Mantel's Cromwell tells us, he shed no lustre of his own, but spun in the reflected light of his master – if it moved, he was gone.

Mantel's trilogy casts Cromwell across multiple reflections. Even Cromwell notes, there have been so many versions he doesn't always recognize himself. But somewhere between fact and fiction there is the real Cromwell: Putney boy, statesman, politician, henchman, father, loyal servant and loyal minister. If we are to learn anything from Mantel's writing it is that beneath every history is indeed another history, and each one deserves to be told.

FURTHER READING

Bernard, G. W., *Fatal Attractions* (London: Yale University Press, 2010)

Bernard, G. W., *Power & Politics in Tudor England* (London: Ashgate, 2000)

Block, J. S., *Factional Politics and the English Reformation 1520–1540* (London: Royal Historical Society, 1993)

Borman, Tracy, *Thomas Cromwell: The Untold Story of Henry VIII's Most Faithful Servant* (London: Hachette, 2014)

Brewer, J. S. and R. H. Brodie, *Letters and Papers, Foreign and Domestic, of the Reign of Henry VIII* (London: HMSO, 1862–1920)

Ellis, Henry, *Original Letters, illustrative of English history: including numerous royal letters, from autographs in the British Museum, and one or two other collections. 2 and 3 series, 11 vols* (London: Richard Bentley, 1824–46)

Elton, Geoffrey, *England under the Tudors* (London: Routledge, 1991)

Everett, Michael, *The Rise of Thomas Cromwell: Power and Politics in the Reign of Henry VIII, 1485–1534* (New Haven: Yale University Press, 2015)

Fraser, Antonia, *The Wives of Henry VIII* (New York: Vintage Books, 1993)

Froude, James Anthony, *Henry VIII and the Reformation* (London: Masters, 1856)

Gunn, Steven, *Henry VII's New Men and the Making of Tudor England* (Oxford: Oxford University Press, 2016)

Gwyn, Peter J., *The King's Cardinal: The Rise and Fall of Thomas Wolsey* (Pimlico, 1992)

Haigh, Christopher, *English Reformations, Religion Politics and Society Under the Tudors* (Oxford: Oxford University Press, 1993)

Hall, Edward, *Halls chronicle; containing the history of England, during the reign of Henry the Fourth, and the succeding monarchs, to the end of the reign of Henry the Eighth, in which are particularly described the manners and customs of those periods. Carefully collated with the editions of 1548–1550* (London: J. Johnson, 1809)

Ives, Eric, *The Life and Death of Anne Boleyn* (London: Blackwell Publishing, 2004)

Lipscomb, Suzannah, *A Visitor's Companion to Tudor England* (London: Ebury Press, 2012)

MacCulloch, Diarmaid, *The Reign of Henry VIII: Politics, Policy, and Piety* (London: Palgrave Macmillan, 1995)

MacCulloch, Diarmaid, *Thomas Cromwell: A Life* (London: Penguin, 2018)

Mackay, Lauren, *Inside the Tudor Court: Henry VIII and his Six Wives through the eyes of the Spanish Ambassador* (Stroud, Amberley, 2015)

Mackay, Lauren, *Among the Wolves of Court: The Untold Story of Thomas and George Boleyn* (London: Bloomsbury Academic, 2018)

Marshall, Peter, *Heretics and Believers: A History of the English Reformation* (New Haven and London: Yale University Press, 2017)

Mattingly, Garrett, *Catherine of Aragon* (Boston: Little, Brown, 1941)

North, John, *The Ambassador's Secret, Holbein and the World of the Renaissance* (Bloomsbury Academic, 2005)

Norton, Elizabeth, *The Lives of Tudor Women* (Head of Zeus, 2016)

Scarisbrick, J. J., *Henry VIII* (Berkeley and Los Angeles: University of California Press, 1968)

Starkey, David, *Six Wives: The Queens of Henry VIII* (London: Random House, 2004)

Williams, Penry, *The Tudor Regime* (Oxford: Clarendon Press, 1979)

Weir, Alison, *The Six Wives of Henry VIII* (New York: Random House, 1993)

INDEX

ACKNOWLEDGEMENTS

I was thrilled when I was first approached to write this companion, for I have been a fan of Hilary Mantel's *Wolf Hall* trilogy from the beginning, even when her versions of historical characters didn't quite match mine. This has been a project like no other, but an utterly rewarding one, to write the history alongside a work of fiction so artfully crafted that even after countless readings I am still drawn to the world Mantel has created. This book has been an absolute joy to write, for the fictional characters as well as their historical counterparts have led such extraordinary lives. So many characters have flitted across my desk throughout the writing process, each demanding their moment, and I have tried to do justice to them all. As a young student I struggled with history's unsavoury version of Thomas Cromwell, but I am thankful to those historians who rescued him from historical ignominy, by presenting him as more than just a 'thug in a doublet:' in particular Geoffrey Elton, Michael Everett, Tracy Borman, but especially Diarmaid MacCulloch. But I think they can all agree Cromwell has had his moment at last.

I must also thank my wonderful agent, Donald Winchester, for thinking of me when the project was first envisioned, and for his constant support and encouragement. I have been fortunate to have a fantastic team at Pavilion/Batsford: John Lee and Tina Persaud who first proposed the project, the irreplaceable Kristy Richardson, whose dedication has made it what it is, as well as Katie Hewett, Gemma Doyle, Claire Clewley, and finally Joanna Lisowiec for her wonderful illustrations.

On a personal note, I must thank my parents, who are long-time fans of Mantel's works, who have savoured every page of her series and have been instrumental in the creation of this companion. And to my husband Klemen, to whom this book is dedicated. You have read so much of Mantel's work, you could likely write your own companion – throughout the journey you have been the most important companion of all.

Also my thanks to Alison Bury, for her constant support and enthusiasm for this project.

And thank you especially to Hilary Mantel, whose formidable trilogy has launched a whole new appreciation of the period. Her prose has been such an influence on my own writing, as I have sought to rehabilitate some of the most maligned individuals of the Tudor age. She has been at my side for so many years, always whispering 'consider this'.